Specter Spectacular
13 Ghostly Tales

———— ◆ ————

edited by
Eileen Wiedbrauk

World Weaver Press

Published by World Weaver Press
Kalamazoo, Michigan
www.WorldWeaverPress.com

Cover photo by Dan Wiedbrauk

First edition: September 2012

ISBN-13: 978-0615700182

SPECTER SPECTACULAR

CONTENTS

INTRODUCTION

What lies beyond the grave has long intrigued humans. And as a realm of the unknown and immeasurable, it's the natural purview for writers of speculative fiction to explore. And to their credit, horror writers have taken the ghostly tale and raised it to an art.

Within *Specter Spectacular: 13 Ghostly Tales* you'll find an eclectic mix of spirit stories. Where ghost stories often seek to appeal to fans of gothic horror, I hope to do that and much more. To invite in folklorists and contemporary fantasy fans as well as those who enjoy the occasional dose of humor with their specters.

What is life? What is death? It's unknown, uncharted. It's emotion— thrills and fears, laughs and loves. And if there's one thing these thirteen stories share, it's that death isn't what we expected.

—Eileen Wiedbrauk

MY REST A STONE
Amanda C. Davis

We are all in the lifeboat and our noses are full of the salt sea and I am hugging my dolly, like always, when her head wobbles once and falls off. The stringy hair slides through my fingers and right over the side. It rolls away with her curls all waving around in the water and her glass eye winks at me to say ha ha, she is leaving. She is leaving and I am not.

So I scream. I am not as good at screaming as I used to be so sometimes I do it for practice, for When We Are Rescued. I scream for a long time.

Mr Bauman says Will Someone Shut That Child Up.

Mrs Adde says Let Her Scream Perhaps Someone Will Hear.

Be A Brave Girl says Miss Mary who I think has forgotten how to say anything else.

I Do Hope My Husband Found A Lifeboat says Mrs Baron because she says it all the time, just like Miss Mary says Be A Brave Girl until I want to hide my face in her skirt and cry, to be cowardly just for spite.

But I don't. I keep screaming. For practice.

Chins Up Girls says Mr Jenson. He is my favorite because he can still say new things like I can and also he is the only man in the boat except for Mr Bauman. Mr Jenson is also very handsome. And Mr Bauman does not like me.

I do not like Mr Bauman either.

I stop screaming. It only fills my mouth with salt anyway. I smile at Mr Jensen and hug my dolly even though her head might be all the way

1

across the ocean by now.

Unsinkable! says Mrs Goldstein. It is the only word she says and she says it as if she is saying the name of someone she hates. She says it like it is a swear. Unsinkable!

Be A Brave Girl says Miss Mary.

Mr Jensen says Think Of All The Dolls Polly because that is my name Think Of All The Dolls You Will Have When We Are Rescued.

We all used to say When We Are Rescued but then everyone forgot how to speak and now it is a special private game for me and Mr Jensen.

I say You Can See Your Best Girl When We Are Rescued.

Mr Jensen says I Bet Your Mama And Papa Are Waiting For You At The Dock.

I saw Mama in the water and Papa on the broken ship and that is why I stayed in this lifeboat for so long. They told me to stay here Until We Are Rescued. And we have not been rescued yet.

I say Sing A Song Please.

Mr Jensen has a handsome voice. He is not so good at singing like I am not so good at screaming but I still like to hear him so I still ask. He sings Nearer My God To Thee Nearer To Thee and then stops and says We Can Sing When We Are Rescued Now I Should Row.

The oars do not work anymore just like our voices do not work but Mr Jensen likes to row so that is what he does. We all do what we like to do now. Even if that is to say Unsinkable! a lot of times as if we hate someone.

Mr Jensen rows. I hug my dolly with no head. A fish swims up to Mr Bauman and then through the hole in his head where there was an eye. It swims around and comes out his teeth.

I Do Wish Someone Would Rescue Us says Mrs Adde.

Be A Brave Girl says Miss Mary.

We have said I Wish We Were Rescued and Be A Brave Girl so many times that I can't help it, I open my jaw to scream salt-water words even though I stopped screaming ten fifty a hundred years ago I think, when we stopped rowing and started sinking and the sun never rose and we stopped saying Oh God Help and started saying When We Are Rescued.

We do what we like to do, saying Unsinkable! and rowing and screaming, and we do it all day long.

And I think we will do the same thing tomorrow.

ALABASTER
Jamie Rand

———•◆•———

By Ben's watch—which he always kept ten minutes fast, because that was what his father did—it was almost five o'clock when they turned from the pavement and followed the rutted tracks deeper into the forest. His uncle Dave, up in the passenger seat, turned the radio down. Grass hissed against the underside of the Jeep and thin branches skittered against the canvas top. It reminded Ben of the sound his nails made when he'd scratch his leg through his jeans.

When the trail climbed a steep hill his father dropped into second and gunned the engine. Ben felt his stomach lurch as the Jeep pitched backwards. Pennies and dimes tumbled from the ashtray and rolled under the seats. A quarter bumped against Ben's shoe and he wiggled down to pick it up.

Dave turned around to look at him. "Almost there, Benny. Excited?"

"Hell yes!" he said, slipping the quarter into his pocket. And then, almost immediately: "Sorry for cussing, Dad."

His father either didn't hear him or elected not to; his eyes were on the road, such as it was. It took a hairpin turn—Ben saw the ground drop away outside his window—and climbed at an even steeper angle. His father downshifted into first. The engine roared like a bear ready to charge. Ben could smell exhaust and burning oil.

"I think we were just about your age when your grandpa first took us here," Dave said. He had to almost shout to be heard over the motor. "That right, Mark?"

3

"Yeah," his father answered. "I was twelve, I think. Maybe thirteen. You were ten."

Ben could imagine his uncle that young—his mom often called him a thirty-year-old boy, so that wasn't a huge leap—but his dad? No *sir*. Trying to imagine his father without his beard, without the premature gray in his hair, trying to picture him without the pack of cigarettes in his shirt pocket or with fingers that weren't dirty under the nails? That was like dividing by zero. Mrs. Jankowski had taught him that in class last year. It was impossible.

Dave smiled. But it was strange. Benny had never seen him smile like that before. Tight-lipped, eyebrows up, eyes narrowed. He opened his mouth like he meant to talk but shut it and glanced at Ben's father. Then, like he was making a joke, he blurted, "Your watch working, Benny?"

Before Ben could answer his dad did it for him. "Shut the fuck up about that, Dave."

"It's working fine, Dad," Benny said, confused and a little hurt at the way he'd sworn. It was an Armitron, a digital with two different time settings, a stopwatch, and a display at the top that told him the day, month, and year. Press a button and the face glowed a radioactive green. It even had a little flashlight, small but bright, like they sometimes sold as key rings. It had been a present for his birthday last week. Brand new. Why *wouldn't* it work?

"I'm sure it works," his dad said. He glanced at his brother. "No reason it shouldn't. Right?"

"Right," Dave said. He bit his lower lip. "Sorry, Mark."

They drove the rest of the way in silence.

At the Cabin

At a quarter past five they pulled into a small dirt turnaround. Ben's father turned off the ignition and yanked the parking brake. He opened his door and stepped outside and Ben squeezed out from the back seat. Late afternoon sun—*July* sun, the best kind to Ben's way of thinking—slanted through the trees in thin spokes. Birds chirped and swooped from branch to branch and he saw a pair of squirrels chasing each other around the thick trunk of a tree. Long shadows from the trees rippled across pine needles and ground turned soft and rounded by rain. The leaves between him and the sun were a burst of green, like the sun was making them glow from the inside, but back the way they had come, down in the valley, they were dark. Almost black. Like looking at shadows that moved in the breeze.

Dave joined them. His father lit a cigarette—Ben, who had been looking back down the path, heard the snap of his Zippo—and walked over to the cabin. It was a small building, no bigger than their garage back home, and not tall, either—the place where the walls stopped and the roof began was only a few inches above his father's head. The walls themselves were all logs, chinked with mud and something Ben didn't know the name for (oakum, his father told him later that night) and the roof was covered in wood shingles, but more than a few of them were missing. A rusty stovepipe stabbed out from one wall and angled up like someone's arm. An old Maxwell House coffee can covered the end of it. Off to one side, a cord of split wood stood squat and fat and somehow sad.

"Doesn't look too bad," his father said. "Thought for sure it'd be ruined."

"The weather?" Dave asked.

"Nah. Hunters. Kids. Kinda surprised no one trashed the place. When's the last time we were here? Six years ago?"

"*You* were," Dave said. "Dad came up here and you went with him. Last time *I* was here, gas was still a dollar." He turned and looked at Ben. "Your grandpa built this place all by himself. Pretty cool, huh?"

"Yeah," Ben said, smiling. It *was*. He walked over to a window and tried to look in, but the glass was so dirty and streaked he couldn't make out anything inside. One pane had a long crack running through it.

His father went to the Jeep and opened the back and took out his rifle. It was an AR-15, Ben knew (and knew too that he was gonna be allowed to shoot it this weekend, so long as he was good; it was another birthday present). He remembered when his dad had bought it—his mom had been mad, *pissed* even, but Uncle Dave had laughed when he heard. "What do you need a fucking M-16 for?" Dave had asked. "Why not a .22 or somethin?" And his father, quiet and shy and very much unlike him, had answered, "It's the only gun I know how to use. Well, that and the SAW. But you can't exactly buy those, and they're kind of overkill for being out in the woods, don't you think?"

Ben didn't know what saws had to do with guns, but he did know that the M-16 (or the AR-15, whatever it was) was the kind of gun his dad had used in the Army. Now, squinting against the cigarette smoke, Mark slapped a magazine into the rifle, just like in the movies, and slung it over his shoulder. He looked at Uncle Dave.

"Show Ben the lake," he said. "I want to make sure the place is clean. I about guarantee it's crawling with possums."

Ben wanted to stay and watch, but he knew better than to ask. Instead, he ran over to the Jeep and grabbed his binoculars. He slung the pair of Bushnells around his neck and grabbed his canteen and his Swiss Army Knife and walked back to his uncle. "Ready?"

"Not like you are, kiddo," he said, laughing. "But sure. Come on."

They had just started down the path when Ben's dad said, quietly, "David?"

"Yeah?"

"Make sure he says on this side."

"I will," he said.

By the Lake

It took them almost fifteen minutes to wind their way down the path. It was steep and thick with big flat rocks that had come loose from the soil ("Your grandpa's idea of a stairway," Dave said, "But he'd probably cry to see it now, don't you think?"). The entire way Ben kept his ears open for the sound of the rifle—the pop like firecrackers—but it never came. He wasn't sure if he felt happy or disappointed about that. He wanted to see his dad shoot it, but if the cabin was clean, if there weren't any possums or rats or anything else cool inside, that meant they'd have more bullets to shoot tomorrow, and that was fine with him.

When they came to the lake, though, he forgot all about it. The lake lay nestled in a perfect bowl of a valley, the water still and quiet and shimmering with the late afternoon sun. Cattails stood around the shoreline like sentries on guard. A small dock jutted out into the water and there was even a boat, upside down, tied to one of the poles.

"I can't believe that thing's still here," Dave said, smiling a little. "I remember taking it out into the water when I was your age."

"Can we go tomorrow?"

"Maybe. If your dad says we can. That's assuming there isn't a hole in the bottom of it. Oh, and if we can find the oars. If they aren't in the cabin, I got no idea where they'd be."

"We could make new ones!"

"Maybe," Dave said. But from the tone of his voice Ben knew he thought it was a dumb idea. Maybe it was. They hadn't brought any tools, except for his own knife, and whittling new oars would take forever. Ben bit his lip, wishing he'd kept his mouth shut, raised his binoculars to his eyes, adjusted the focus, and looked out over the far side of the lake.

He had to squint against the sun shining down from his right, but he saw a lot. Fish dimpling the water. A flight of birds taking off from the upper branches of an old and twisted tree. He made out oaks and maples and a few other kinds of trees he knew from his Audubon book. And—weird—he saw a patch of land about halfway up the other slope that looked brown and dark and dead, like there had been a fire. The trees in it were black, as if they were covered in soot, entirely bare of leaves. Their branches stuck out like huge thorns.

Ben sat down and crossed his legs and put his elbows on his knees, like he had seen his father do. He raised the binoculars and rolled the focus wheel just a little. And there, inside that strange dead patch, he saw an old building, maybe another cabin. There was no roof, but Ben could see beams where it should have been. They were gray and curved and made him think of rib bones.

Alabaster, he thought, for no reason at all. It was a word he had no way of knowing and to his mind's voice it sounded deep and guttural and somehow alien.

"Uncle Dave?" he asked. "What's that?"

He paused before he answered. "What's what."

Ben handed the binoculars up. "Just a little above the lake. There's a big tree. Behind that. You see it? It looks like there was a fire, or something. There's a building, too."

Dave looked through the binoculars for a long time. Ben glanced up at him, confused. He'd gone still.

"Ben," he said.

"Yeah?"

"Your watch *is* working, right?"

He looked down at it. It read 5:37. "Sure. Why? What's wrong?"

He sighed, squatted down next to Ben, and handed him the binoculars. "Nothing. Not a thing. But I want you to make me a promise, okay? Two promises. First, don't go over there. Stay on this side of the lake. Like your dad said."

"Why? What is it?"

He snapped, "Just trust me on this one, okay? Please?"

Ben looked down at the binoculars, embarrassed. The compass built into it pointed almost perfectly north. He ran his thumb over it, trying to bite back sudden tears. Dave never yelled at him. Not even when Ben accidentally hit a baseball into the side of his car last year, denting the fender, costing him a hundred bucks and causing Ben a month of indentured servitude mowing his lawn as payment. "Sure, Uncle Dave."

"The other promise. If your watch stops working, you tell me or your dad right away. Or—wait. Do you have a phone yet?"

"No. Mom won't let have one until I'm thirteen."

"Okay, that's fine. Nevermind that. Just the watch. Okay?"

"Sure," he said, more confused than ever.

"Good," Dave said. He glanced over the lake and his eyes narrowed. But then he looked over at Ben and smiled. "Think your dad's done scaring the possums away?"

"Probably."

"Think you might want to learn how to build a fire? How to stack tinder and kindling?"

"What's tinder?"

"Small stuff. Leaves, dry bark. Belly button lint."

"Belly button lint?"

"Nothin catches as fast as that," Dave said sagely. "It's gross, but it works. You'll see. Wanna learn?"

"Sure!" Ben said. He stood up and dusted off his pants. His uncle started up the hill and he followed behind. But he couldn't stop a glance back at that strange and somehow frightening dead area on the far side of the lake.

Around the Cooler

When they returned to the cabin (both of them breathing heavily, and Dave more than a little red in the face), Ben found his father pulling their stuff out of the back of the Jeep. He saw their tent there with their packs and the cooler and the rifle and knew they wouldn't be sleeping inside.

"No possums," Mark said. "No raccoons, either. But the place is birdshit central. They crapped over *everything*."

"Charming," Dave said. "Guess we're under the stars tonight?"

"Yeah. I'm gonna set up the tent in case it rains. Ben? Want to help?"

"Uncle Dave said he'd show me how to start a fire."

"Did he?"

"With belly button lint," Dave said, smiling. "I'll help with the tent, Mark. Hey, Benny?"

"Yeah?"

"I want you to go find some stones. Gotta make a fire ring before we can make a fire, you know."

"How many?"

"Seven or eight, I guess. Big ones." He held out his hand, fingers apart. "About that big. Think you can do that?"

"Sure!"

"Don't go too far, now. You should be able to find some pretty close."

"Okay," he said. He went off with his hands in his pockets, the binoculars bouncing against his chest, lips puckered, trying to whistle notes that wouldn't come. He found a good-sized rock under a leaning pine and wiggled it back and forth, working it loose from the soil. He thought of teeth and rotten gums and made a face. That was kinda gross.

When he had it free he picked it up and started back toward the cabin. The Jeep was between him and his father and he crept up to it, slow and quiet. He wanted to listen in (*eavesdrop* was the word; it had been on his last vocabulary test) and hear if they said anything about shooting the gun tomorrow.

Ben put the rock down and squatted behind the right rear tire. He rose up a little and through the windows he could see his dad and his uncle unrolling the tent. When they had it laid out, Dave opened the cooler and pulled out a couple of beers. He flicked icy water from the ends of his fingers and handed one of the cans to Mark, who cracked it open and drank deep. He belched and asked, "How'd Ben like the lake?"

"Fine," Uncle Dave answered. The smile slipped from his mouth and he lowered his voice. Ben could barely hear. "The hut's there, Mark. He saw it with his binoculars."

"What?"

"I swear to God, man."

"David, we burned that fucking place down."

"That's the thing. The *trees* still looked burned. There's no grass. But the cabin's there."

"That was twenty years ago. Shit woulda grown back."

"Go see for yourself, if you want," Dave said. "I'm not shittin you. Was it like that last time you came?"

"Six years ago? I don't know. We didn't have time to see. Dad started feeling bad the night we got here. We turned around and went home. Didn't even unpack."

Dave wiped his hand down his face and sat down on the cooler. Ben could see his shirt, splotchy with sweat, sticking to his back. "I hate to say it but, you know, we should probably do the same."

Mark took another drink of his beer. "I can't. Ben'd be disappointed. This is his birthday present. As long as he stays away from the hut, he'll be fine. You remember."

"The place fucking … *grew* back, Mark. You remember what was inside."

He closed his eyes and tilted his head back and sighed. When he looked at Dave again, Ben thought, he seemed suddenly old. Worse than old. Tired. *Worn.*

"Look," Mark said. "Things aren't good with me and Nikki right now, okay? Part of why I came here with Ben was to get me out of the house. I can't face her right now, man. She's got a lot going on and all I'm doing is fucking things up. All right? If we go back and Ben tells her we stayed at a hotel or something, she'd be *pissed* at me. I need that like I need a fucking hole in the head."

Dave sipped at his beer. "Sorry. I didn't know."

"It's fine," Mark said. He fumbled the pack of cigarettes out of his shirt pocket and lit one. "Look. Sorry I snapped at you. I'll keep Ben busy tomorrow. Gonna show him the rifle. That'll probably take all day. Then we leave Sunday morning. Everything'll be fine."

"Sure," Dave said.

"Now are you gonna help me with the tent, or what?"

"Another beer first?"

"Fuck," Mark said, leaning against the Jeep. "Why not."

Ben crept away silently.

Beside the Fire

Belly button lint didn't actually start that fire (they didn't have enough of it, anyway, and when Ben went spelunking all he came back with was a gross-smelling finger), but pine needles, dead leaves, and dry bark did. Uncle Dave, smelling a little like beer, showed him how to make a small pile of tinder under a teepee of twigs. He even let Ben light it.

They sat around the circle of stones Ben had made for the fire pit (more an oval than a circle, really, but Uncle Dave said that was fine) while the night crept in around them. Ben's father pulled some raw hamburger out of the cooler and wrapped it in tinfoil—to Ben, it looked like the world's biggest Hershey's Kiss—and cooked it low in the coals. They ate the meat out of hotdog buns with ketchup and mustard. Ben had an unbelievable three, while his father and his uncle put down five a piece, drinking beer all the while and throwing their empty cans into the fire.

Nine o'clock was his usual bedtime and throughout the evening he kept looking at his watch as it drew closer, sure that come the time his father would shuffle him off into the sleeping bag. But it came and went and Ben said nothing, feeling happy, feeling *proud*, that they let him stay up. He knew his chances of staying up even longer would be better if he said as little as possible, and so he sat in front of the fire, quiet and still.

Dave stood, stretched, and yawned. Mark, his eyes gone glazed with beer, looked up at him and smiled. Ben scooted closer to the fire and wrapped his arms around his legs. It was getting chilly.

"I'm off to bed," his uncle announced. "Bag. Whatever." He walked to the Jeep and reached into the back seat and pulled out an old lantern. It was one of the kind that took the big square batteries, Ben knew. It'd been in his father's garage for years, hanging just above the workbench.

"Puttin the flashlight on the hood," he said. "Case anyone wakes up and has to pee, up to and including me. Knowing my luck I'd step wrong and go face-first all the way to the lake."

"Thanks, Dave," his father said.

"No problem. Thanks for bringing me along. This is pretty nice. *Great* night. Lookit all those *stars*."

"Yeah," his dad agreed, smiling. Ben smiled, too. It was good to see him do that. Back home there hadn't been very many lately. He and Ben's mother never argued (at least not in front of Ben), but over the last six months, since just past Christmas, there'd been *silences*. Short answers. Hurt looks that no one but Ben saw. It was worse than fighting. At least *then* they'd talk to each other. The unhappy and somehow lonesome quiet was like a monster all of them saw but none of them talked about, and Ben had no idea how to fight it. He didn't even know if he *could*.

Things aren't good with me and Nikki right now, okay?

"You all right, Benny?"

He looked over at his dad as Dave walked between. "Yep. Just being quiet. Thinking."

"What about?"

You and Mama, he thought. "Nothing," he lied.

"Long face for nothing."

He forced himself to smile. "This was a great birthday, Dad. That's what I was thinking. Thanks."

His father gave him a sidelong glance. "Think you'd want to shoot the gun tomorrow?"

Ben already knew, of course. But he couldn't let his dad know that. "Really?"

"Really. Tomorrow morning I'll teach you how to use it. *Safely*, that's the important thing. There're some rules you need to learn. If you can do that, probably after lunch I'll set you up some targets. See how you do."

"Great, Dad. Thanks."

"There's a trade-off, though. Know what it is?"

Ben knew where this was going. He'd heard his father make this deal before. "You want me to go to bed, right?"

"Yep. We have to get up early if we want to shoot."

Ben didn't argue, not when they were already up late. "Okay. What about the fire?"

"It's low enough. Let it burn out. It'll keep the skeeters away."

"Okay." Ben stood and went over to his sleeping bag and sat down and took off his shoes. No pajamas, not out here; here he slept in his clothes like guys were supposed to. He wiggled into the cold bag down deep so that only his head stuck out.

For a while he watched the fire. Watched his father nurse another beer before crumpling the can and throwing it inside the stones where it lay hissing against the coals. After that Ben turned onto his side and looked out at the woods that surrounded them. The moon above was full and fat and he thought he could see all the way down to the water.

Later, he heard his father climb into his own sleeping bag. Not long after that, he was snoring.

Down the Path

A little past midnight, lying sleepless in his bag, staring up at the moon as it shifted down through the trees, Ben had started thinking about the hut. No reason, really; the thought wasn't there, and then, suddenly, it was. He started thinking about how his uncle had warned him away from the place. About how his father wanted them to stay on this side of the lake. It seemed to Ben that adults just didn't want to face things. To deal with things. It was like they put up some kind of fence around the problem and just ignored it. But you couldn't do that. His father had told him so lots of times. The best thing to do was to face it.

So why wasn't his dad doing just that? Why couldn't he just take Mom out to the movies or something, out to dinner, and talk? Ben was old enough to not need a babysitter; he'd happily watch the house if they wanted to go have fun. But no. They weren't talking. They were afraid.

And the hut, Ben was afraid of that, the way they were afraid to talk. Which was why he wanted to go see it. To prove that what his father had told him was true, that you had to deal with your fears. And maybe, come tomorrow, he'd tell his dad what he had done, tell him that if he, Ben, a *kid*, could do it, there was no reason his father couldn't. And maybe things would be better at home. Maybe they'd talk to each other again. Smile at each other again. Most kids said it was gross when their parents kissed (and even grosser when you thought they had to *do it*, at least once, to have had you), but Ben didn't feel that way. If the option was the silence or the kisses, the kisses won every time.

He slowly unzipped his sleeping bag, his eyes shifting back and forth between the shapeless form of his father, on the far side of the dead fire, and his uncle, close by. Every noise—the slow plastic click of the zipper, the sharp whisper of the nylon—seemed incredibly loud and he was sure they'd wake up. If they did, he'd say he had to pee.

But they slept on, oblivious.

Ben slipped his shoes on and tiptoed to the Jeep, where he cracked open the door and grabbed his Swiss Army Knife. The compass on the binoculars was detachable—a quarter turn to the left and off it came. In his palm it looked like a glass eye with a slit pupil. He put it in his pocket, shivering away the image. He didn't think he'd get lost, not with the lake to guide him, but better to have it. Safer.

He started down the path. Up here, away from the city and under the full moon, the night was brighter than he ever imagined it could be, bright enough to throw shadows, dim as they were. He could hear frogs clicking and croaking down by the lake and the entire world seemed filled with the sound of crickets, above him, below him, to every side. He heard the soft grind of his sneakers against the soil. Ahead of him the path wound down between the trees like a dead snake. Beyond that, he knew, it followed the shoreline. And after that, on the far side, was the hut.

The boat glinted in the night, not far away now. The moon ran over its metal skin and down its sides like water. As he walked past, something small and quick darted out from beneath it and went scurrying into the brush. The grass rustled as it swallowed the animal and then stood still.

I'm not really doing this, Ben thought remotely. Sweat had broken out on his face despite the night's chill. It felt like ice against his forehead. *I could turn around and go back. Right now. If they see me I'll just say I had to pee and got lost.*

His body jerked that way, as if something were pulling him on strings. He even took a first step back toward the camp. But then he thought of what his father had said. Worse, the way he had said it.

I can't face her right now, man. She's got a lot going on and all I'm doing is fucking things up.

I'll fix that, Ben thought. *This will fix that.*

Slowly, he turned back toward the lake and followed the path. He checked his watch, squinting against the square of bright green light. It read 12:28.

Outside the Hut

When he stepped into the dead circle that surrounded the building he felt suddenly dizzy. Lightheaded. His heart pounded in his chest like it meant to burst free and he felt a sudden and almost desperate urge to urinate. Then the feeling passed almost as quickly as it came and he stood, blinking away tears, swallowing his fear, thinking of his father.

Ben stopped just before the cabin. It jutted up in front of him like something raised from the earth, a skeleton not yet wrapped in flesh. The archway leading inside gaped at him, a black mouth with teeth long rotted and fallen away. The joists and rafters of the roof that had been gray in the sunlight were now the alabaster of bones bleached long years.

Alabaster, he thought. And then, *What does that even mean?*

He walked closer. There was a smell here. Not the wet musk of the lake or the Christmas smell of the pines. This was worse. It made him think of rotting orchards, where apples went sickly sweet in their decay. Of the strange electric smell of his uncle's train set. Of the way his grandmother smelled her final and painful days in the hospital.

A low gibbering sound came from the darkness inside the doorway. A throaty laugh thick with saliva. *A frog,* he thought hysterically. *A frog, it got lost, found its way up here, no big deal, I mean, come on, Benny, it's nothing, there's a ton of them down there, you can hear them—*

But no. He *couldn't* hear them. Or the crickets, which he had listened to all night long. They had faded every step he took farther inside this dead space. His fear, his terror, had deafened him to it, and now he stood in a place so quiet the only sound left, the only *natural* sound, was the placental beating of his heart.

It's dark inside, he realized suddenly. *There's no roof and it's dark.*

Slowly, as if his arm wasn't even his, he raised his wrist. He meant to use the small but bright flashlight in the watch to look inside. That was what he'd do. Look inside, see the frog, see the nothing, turn around, go back.

But his hands, trembling as they were, found the wrong button. When the screen lit up he screamed. The light, usually bright, was the dead sickly yellow of plaque-thick teeth. According to the digital readout, it was 13:94 on Friday, May 63rd, 1246.

The sound from the hut came again, louder, washing over him, ripping his skin into shivers. He jabbed into his pocket for his knife and yanked it out, feeling the little lips of the blades with his shaking fingers, looking for the notch for his thumbnail. The compass fell out of his pocket and landed face up. It swung toward magnetic north for a brief moment before pivoting like a metronome keeping a perfect beat.

When it stepped into the moonlight, Ben's first thought, distant and clinical, was of his grandfather. A short, shriveled shape. *A ghost*, he thought. Faint. So faint. *This is what they look like. This is what they really are.*

When it raised its head and looked at him, his urine broke. He felt it splash across his testicles and into his underwear and down his legs. The thing was smiling. The corners of its mouth reached to where its ears would have been, had it any. Its teeth, far too big for its face, were the twisted and conical shape of ancient stalactites. Its tongue capered inside its maw and pushed out through its smile like hamburger through a grinder.

The knife fell from numb hands. The thing staggered toward him, loping like an ape. Against the black and burned soil it left no marks.

Ben turned and bolted. His lungs pulled in the stink of this dead hot place and puked it back out. The big muscles in his thighs knotted in pain. But worst was the ache in his guts, the nausea of half-digested meat. It felt like it was rotting in his stomach.

When the thing caught him by the shoulder and yanked him backwards, his legs flew out from beneath him and he landed badly. When it grabbed him by the hair and started dragging him effortlessly back into the hut, he began vomiting. Writhing on his shirt among the miscarriage of hamburger and bread were small worms like maggots.

Alabaster

Dave woke up to piss away his beer when he noticed Benny was gone.

"Ben?" he called. "Hey, Benny?"

No answer. None but the crickets, and even they seemed disinterested.

His first thought was the hut, of course. And of the thing he and Mark had glimpsed inside it twenty years ago. They'd gone down to see it, the both of them. A night not all that different from this one. They'd gotten close to the place. Closer than they should have been. Their flashlights had stopped working, he remembered that. And when he had looked at his watch, nothing was there but an impossible, obscene time. He had never worn a watch since, and Mark, not long after, had taken up smoking.

Dave leaned down and shook his brother awake. The eyes that peered up at him were red-rimmed and swollen.

"Mark," he said. "Wake up. Ben's gone."

The last words arrowed through his fog of beer and sleep. He sat up almost instantly, eyes wide with sudden adrenaline. "The rifle," he said. "Where's the rifle?"

"By the Jeep. I'll get the flashlight. Don't forget your boots."

Dave heard the slingshot sound of the gun as his brother chambered a round. A minute later they were running down to the lake, the light from the lantern pinwheeling crazily over the soil. He almost fell twice, once tripping over a root, the other because he missed one of the old stone steps. Mark caught him both times.

They had burned the fucking place down. They *had*. Their father had been asleep in his cabin that second night. They'd gone back with the small, oil-stained gas can that held fuel for the chainsaw. They got as close as they dared, flinging gas at the backside of the building. Mark had lit a wad of paper with his father's lighter and tossed it. They'd run, not caring if the whole fucking forest caught fire. And of course it hadn't. Not when the flames twisted slowly in the strange air around that place, when they licked down instead of up and burned violet. They'd run back to the dock and stood hand-in-hand, listening to it smolder. It screamed like something dying.

It had stormed that night, he remembered. Not long after their arson. The next day, when their father saw the blackened ruins where the hut stood, he'd nodded. Later he blamed the lightning, but at that moment he knew the truth. And about it, he had said nothing.

At the shoreline, he and Mark almost missed Ben. They turned to the right, meaning to run the entire way to the hut, the fucking hut, when Dave happened to glance to his left, toward the dock. And there he saw Ben, standing on its edge, looking out across the lake, the same place

Dave had stood with his brother twenty years before.

"Mark," he said. He pointed. "Look. *Ben! Hey Benny!*"

He turned toward them and waved.

His father was the first one to reach him. He dropped the rifle and knelt before his son and wrapped him in his arms. Dave, years out of shape and forty pounds overweight, stood where he had first seen Ben, his hands on his hips, pulling in deep lungfuls of air. Even from this distance, thirty feet or more, he could hear Mark saying, "Jesus, Ben, oh Jesus Christ, you scared the living shit out of me."

Ben stood there, smiling. Dazed, even. In the moonlight he looked young. Young and frail. Dave stood and made to walk toward him when the flashlight flickered and died.

And from his nephew's young mouth came the voice of something old, ancient, something far older than they, older than their race, maybe as old as the earth.

Alabaster, it said, a word Dave had forgotten he'd ever known, before it raised its child's hands and plunged its thumbs into its father's eyes. The fingers sunk into the back of his skull more than knuckle deep and squeezed. Mark had time to let out one short and brutish scream before it tore his face apart and held aloft fistfuls of bone and brain and hair like trophies. When it turned to look at him, Dave dropped the flashlight and ran.

He stumbled up the path, hands scrabbling for purchase, his breath sawing sharp pains through his throat and lungs. He looked back once, crying in fear and horror, and saw it capering after him.

When Dave made it to the cabin he dove into the Jeep like a man running for a foxhole. He slammed the door and reached down to start the ignition and remembered, too late, that Mark had the keys. A sudden shape stood at the window and he turned, hopeless, to look.

Benny was smiling. The smile reached up well past his ears and into his hairline. And there, in that inhuman grimace, David saw the teeth he remembered, the sharpened spikes of them, too many, like they filled his whole mouth.

I burned, it said. *I burned.*

Alabaster.

Alabaster.

Alabaster.

CINDER
Kristina Wojtaszek

———————◆———————

Beyond the rhythmic rasp of his own breath, Edan could hear the house cry out in death. Rafters buckled and snapped behind him, piercing through the hiss of water from the live line his buddies had dragged in. They were battling the beast at ground level while he searched the second floor. He struggled down the hall where he'd heard whimpering a moment ago, then ripped off his mask in a last effort to see the door more clearly. Soot-blackened tears fell and his lungs heaved, rejecting the toxic air; his whole body was racked with pain as he coughed out smoke. Embers, like tiny fairies, burst into wild flight as he threw his body into the door. His daughter would see things like that—find beauty in the midst of hell. He choked on the thought and took a draw of oxygen from his mask once more. Why, when the roof was disintegrating and the rooms he'd traveled through to get here were nothing more than a gaping inferno, was this damn door so stubborn? Parting his thoughts like a curtain was his little girl. If she only knew what lay beyond the door … Finally, his boot buckled its center, shards snapping, releasing a cool draft from the broken window inside. Glass littered the floor, a thousand stars reflecting heat. There she was. He'd expected her to be bigger, but then, everyone who crumpled and slept from smoke inhalation looked small and deflated. He couldn't see her sides heave. He strained, ran his gloved hand along her charred fur, feeling for life. He lifted her gently, her head hanging limp over his shoulder, and started carefully back down the hall. From another room he yelled down, and a ladder was shifted over to him. Heading down through the starless night, he could hear his comrades shouting and clapping above the wails of an ambulance.

He could see she was gone as he laid her down on the ambulance floor; still, the attendants worked on her, slipping an oxygen mask over her muzzle. "Sorry, girl," he whispered. Looking away, he saw Officer Taldon questioning the family. He stepped near to hear the sobbing woman. "It's my fault. I had her shut in that room … She was my husband's dog, before we met. After he died, I … I couldn't stand to look at her. I tried to give her to friends, but no one could take her or wanted her. I even drove her to the pound, but I couldn't do it. I knew he'd hate me for that. We used to keep her outside all the time, in the back, but …" she broke off, weeping.

One of the two teenage girls who stood holding her mother's hand spoke up, "There was some stray runnin' around—a boy dog. She was always trying to run off with him and we didn't want her to get pregnant. She even dug under the fence and got out one time. So mom had to start keepin' her in the house. She had her own room, with a dog bed and water and food and stuff. We'd take her for walks when we got home from school and love on her, but we just couldn't leave her out like we used to." Tears glistened in her eyes as well.

"Wasn't she spayed?" Taldon asked.

The mother shook her head, collecting herself. "My husband didn't believe in that. He said it was cruel." She shrugged, "I didn't want to go against his wishes." Edan turned away before they noticed him and strode back to the ambulance. Poor, unwanted creature. If they managed to save her, he'd adopt her himself. He almost smiled, thinking how much his daughter would like that. But as he approached, the EMT shook her head sadly. "Damn." He ran his hand over the lab's head, rubbing behind her ears reflexively. His fingers brushed her tag, a small flash of silver in his dirty palm. It read:

Princess
Daddy's Girl
Roger Byrd

There was a phone number and address on the back side. His heart squeezed at the sight of her name, the same pet name he often called his daughter by. Mrs. Byrd was standing beside him suddenly, sniffing back her tears. The EMT squeezed her shoulder in way of apology, "Sure was a pretty girl. Sorry we couldn't do more."

Edan eyed Mrs. Byrd, "What will you do with her?"

She shrugged, "We really can't afford much, especially now …"

He ran a hand through his hair, sending a rain of ash to his shoulders; a fireman's dandruff. "Was your husband buried here in town?"

She shook her head, "Cremated. I kept the ashes."

"Mind if I take her?"

The woman raised her brows, "What?"

"I can see to it she's buried properly—I've got a nice spot under a shady tree in our backyard. Unless you want her ashes, too."

"Oh." She shook her head, "No. If you'd like to bury her, I'd be grateful." The woman turned, wandering back to her daughters without any further goodbye.

This time, when he lifted her, she felt as light and featureless as a throw. He wondered where he'd keep her until he could get a hole dug. Maybe in the shed, where his daughter wouldn't find her. He almost laughed at the thought of an urn in that smoldering house. Wouldn't that be something, incinerated twice over. Being a firefighter, if only part-time, that was one thing Edan knew he didn't want. Bury him in the cool earth; he'd had enough of fire.

Ron came up and slapped him on the back before noticing that the dog was lifeless in his arms. "Shit. One casualty after all."

Edan could do little more than nod.

"Hey, Flash, why don't you head on home. You've been out here all night. We'll clean up."

Edan smiled his relief and walked off among the blue and red phantoms cast by the ambulance quietly rolling away into the night. A light rain had aided in drowning out the last of the fire and the yellow warning tape had been hung around the property's perimeter. Reports would be filed in office the next morning. Hell, it was probably already morning, Edan thought, as he felt the weight of exhaustion pull at his limbs. He had a short walk back to the station where he'd parked his sedan earlier. The damp asphalt glistened and winked under the dull street lights, storm drains gurgling at his heals. He was thinking of water-logged cemeteries and shoveling up mud in his backyard when a fierce ache in his forearms caused him to stop and shift the dog's weight. She shifted back, squirming suddenly, half-leaping, half-falling to the wet ground. She lay there for a moment as he stared at her water-spiked coat, adrenaline feeding hasty explanations to his brain. He jumped as she huffed and sneezed out a bit of choking soot. She rose unsteadily, her hind quarters unnaturally slumped, and blinked at him through the rain.

"Daddy, my tummy's hungry. I want some smiley-side eggs!" Edan grinned even as he clung to the soft, gray slumber that misted his mind. This must be what a stuffed animal feels like, he mused, all fluff and comfort, half awakened by a child's love. He pulled his daughter up into the tall bed with him, squeezing her tight. She squirmed, giggling, and he remembered how the dog had squirmed out of his arms ... He stiffened, his eyes fully focused, though his voice still scratched like dry tinder, "Ok, Baby Girl, go on upstairs, I'll make your eggs. You sure you want sunny-side up and not scrambled? Last time you liked the scrambled with ketchup."

"Smiley-side, smiley-side!" she chanted, bouncing up and down on her toes. He smirked then winced, his chapped lips splitting.

As he placed her eggs before her at the kitchen table he knelt and said, "Baby, what would you name a princess, if you found one?"

"Did you find one, Daddy?"

He nodded somberly and she took on his serious demeanor. "Cinderella. She's my favorite. Is she pretty like Mommy?"

He smiled, "She's pretty, but not like Mommy. I'll let you meet her after breakfast. But you have to promise to be brave, okay?"

"Why Daddy? I thought she was a princess? Isn't she good?"

"Yeah, she is; she's a real good girl, but she's ... well, she doesn't feel too good right now. She was in a fire when I found her. She'll be all right though, we just have to take good care of her. Will you help me with that?" The little girl nodded sagely, her eyes larger than the yolks on her plate. He smoothed her sleep-rumpled hair, "I knew you would."

In fact he had checked on the dog several times that night, readjusting a comforter around her, scooting a bowl of fresh water closer to her nose. She'd peeked at him with one eye and whined a little, then sighed heavily and went back to sleep. Before making breakfast he'd snuck a last glance at her and she was lapping up the water at last, her hind end still sprawled under her on the blanket. Darra ran downstairs after eating three bites of her breakfast and waited by the door to the spare room. Edan smiled, ruffling her hair and said, "Go ahead, Princess." She cracked open the door, her face pressed to the gap, and peered in for a moment before throwing it all the way open. "A doggy! Can we keep her, Daddy? Please?" She had her arms looped around the dog's head and the lab was licking her with interest. The thump of her tail caught Edan's attention and he knelt to massage her haunches. "Hmm. First thing, we need to get her feeling better. I'm not sure her back end is doing so well, and she needs to be checked over." His daughter wasn't listening, her face wet with dog kisses as she cooed, "You're my Cinderella. You're my girl, now. I'll take good care of you!"

Edan phoned the vet while Darra coaxed their new pet outside. He explained about the fire; the possibility of respiratory damage and how he thought something heavy may have fallen on her back end. "We'll get her in today, then. And does she have a name?" the receptionist asked.

"Cinderella," he coughed out. Why couldn't his daughter have picked Belle, or Beauty or even Snow White? He just couldn't imagine shouting "Cinderella" for the whole neighborhood to hear. Maybe he could shorten it. As he wrote down the appointment time he glanced up through the sliding glass doors that led to the backyard. Darra was following close behind the lab as she hobbled around the perimeter, sniffing out her new boundaries. She stopped as if aware of his attention, hazel eyes peering at him from the shade of the tree he'd meant to bury her under. He shook his head, staring at her burned off whiskers and her soft gold pelt beneath the charred outer fur. A living cinder, he thought, and shivered at the irony of the name his daughter had chosen.

As the garage door lifted Edan was startled by the sight of a woman standing at the front door. She turned, eyeing him over her Oakleys, and he recognized her as Mrs. Byrd. He smiled around the knot in his gut, wondering if she would want her dog back once she knew. "I brought a couple of Princess's things," she told him. "It's amazing that anything was left after the fire, but ... anyway, here's her old leash and brush and a photo of my husband with her. See, she was just a puppy here." Edan stared down at the picture of a puppy so pale she was almost white with a dark smudge of a nose and a hint of hazel ringing her otherwise coal-black eyes. She was held in the arms of a middle-aged man in a hunting flannel, who smiled over her with pride. Edan looked back up at the man's widow, standing beside him. "I forgot that Roger wanted these things buried with her. But if you've already ..."

"Actually, Mrs. Byrd, I have something to show you." She followed him through the garage to the backyard where Darra was stubbornly tossing a tennis ball to Cinderella. The poor lab hobbled after it with all the strength she could muster, her back legs half dragging, half paddling behind her. Edan smiled at the sight, knowing she had the will to recover. He turned to Mrs. Byrd, still holding the memorabilia in her arms. She glanced at him, then back across the yard. "Um. Oh. Is that the spot, there? Beneath that tree?"

Edan stared at her for a long moment while she watched his daughter with interest. He cleared his throat, "It's a miracle, but she seems to be doing just fine."

Mrs. Byrd was clearly confused. "Oh? Is she your daughter?"

"Yeah, but I meant …"

"She has quite the imagination, doesn't she?"

Edan glanced back to Darra who was holding up the dog's floppy ear to whisper something in it.

"My girls had imaginary friends, too," Mrs. Byrd continued, smiling obligingly. "Anyway, it doesn't look like you've dug her grave yet, so I'd appreciate it if you'd just place these things in with her. Do you mind?"

Edan almost laughed. Maybe she had poor eyesight. He turned to call Cinder to them and choked, his mouth half open as he watched Darra stroking empty air. "Where's … where'd she …" he stammered, looking wildly around the yard. Mrs. Byrd took several steps back as he paled visibly and startled his daughter by yelling. She set the items down on the step and whispered, "I should go. Thank you and … goodbye." No one paid any attention as she hurried away to her car.

"But Daddy, why can't Cinderella come in and be with me?"

Edan carried Darra into the house, locking the sliding glass doors behind them. Dog whines had floated up around them from the empty lawn, and he swore he heard the click of her nails on the glass doors, but he saw nothing. He pulled the curtains shut and dragged Darra downstairs, cursing under his breath as he fumbled with the remote, trying to start a movie for her. Darra was oblivious to his panic. He knelt down, cupping her sweet face in his hand, "Honey, did Cinder, I mean Cinderella … did she look funny to you outside?"

She wrinkled her dark brows, "No. I think she's pretty! Can't she come in and watch a movie with me?"

Edan resisted the urge to run back to the window and check again. Had he lost his mind? Was this some kind of a sick dream? But he'd almost tripped over the things Mrs. Byrd had left behind, and he'd seen a glimpse of her red Mini speed off. She'd acted as though the dog wasn't there, and when he'd looked that second time … she *wasn't*.

"Daddy?"

"No, Sweetie. She can't come in right now, okay?" Her tiny face jiggled in his trembling hand before he dropped it and stood. "How 'bout some popcorn?"

They spent the rest of the day watching movies and playing board games. Darra begged for Cinderella until he finally lied, "I talked to the doggy doctor on the phone, Sweetie, and he said she needs to be left alone outside today so she can get better. I'll check on her in a little while, but she's supposed to rest. In the fresh air. Okay, Honey?" In fact he hadn't bothered to cancel the appointment, but he had called his wife, still out of town at a conference. He lost his words to the choppy connection and gave up, only telling her he couldn't wait for her to come home. Of course she wanted to talk to their daughter so he handed his cell to Darra. "Mommy, we have a new doggy now! I named her Cinderella and she's golden! Do you think she's a real princess?"

Edan sprayed his mouthful of wine all over the kitchen table. "Honey, lemme talk to Mommy ..." He actually laughed when she asked about it, echoing Mrs. Byrd's words, "She's got such a vivid imagination, doesn't she?"

Edan woke with a start, the shout that crouched in his throat tumbling out in little more than a whimper. Darra shifted in her tiny bed as he peeled himself off her bedroom floor. He wandered through the dark house, wincing at the brilliant green display on the microwave. It was past midnight. He decided to check the doors one more time. He'd shut the garage door with the remote earlier, but the door leading from the garage to the backyard was still open. As he slid the chain across the back door, the whining started up again and he fell backwards at the sound of claws scraping at the other side. Her plaintive cries sounded pitifully like the word "ow," and he wondered if she was in pain. Or thirsty. Shit. "All right, girl," he whispered, flipping on the light, "but you damn well better be there!" She pushed her nose against the crack as he eased open the door. He touched it, wet and cold against his fingers as it should be. He opened the door all the way and she staggered, heaving her body over the step. She was damp, her pelt jolting under his hand as he stroked her shivering side. She kept her head low, licking his bare foot. Edan wiped the wet from his eyes and coaxed her upstairs into the kitchen where he set out deli meat and a large mixing bowl full of fresh water. He stared as she limped across the vinyl floor. Her rear end was held higher than before, as if she was finally recovering the strength of her back legs, but something still seemed to hurt. In the light from the refrigerator he saw spots of blood behind her. After she gulped down the food and water, he eased her onto her side and examined her feet. Bits of glass caught the light as he spread apart her pads, most of them red with fresh blood. He kissed her soft ears, whispering his apologies, before leaving her to hunt down a pair of tweezers. When he came back to the kitchen, Darra was there in her Tinker Bell nightgown, snuggled into the crook of Cinder's curled side. She watched with worry as he plucked the shards of glass from her feet. "Did her slippers break in the fire?" Darra asked between yawns.

"What?"

"Her glass slippers, Daddy."

Edan counted slowly as he sucked stale air through his mask, trying to keep his breathing slow. Despite his forced calm his fingers trembled, drumming his quick pulse across the handle of his axe. Shane fell back, doubling over as he battled the smoke that trickled in through his mask. "Crack the hinges!" he managed between ragged breaths. Edan stepped up to swing his axe but stopped, his arms burning above him as he listened. Shane raised his eyes and Edan stared past the flames in his mask to see if he heard it too. Shane nodded, "She's not in here!"

"Where?"

"I don't ..." They strained to hear past the snaps of timber and rush of flame. "Behind us ... Somewhere behind us." Shane shook his head as they stared down the long hall behind them, two doors on each side. "I'm sorry, Flash. I can't ..." He broke into a violent cough.

"Get out of here! Send Ron up. Get some air, now!" Edan shouted and disappeared into the dark hall, sending the call for backup over his portable. A wave of fatigue knocked him senseless as the smoke engulfed him. He could feel the steam rising up from the water on the floor, making him sweat inside his boots. He tested the knob of the first door to his right, watching the paint on the wall bubble and blister beside his face. That one could be hiding a flashover. If he opened it, he might not make it past the inferno to the next door. He backed up as bits of timber fell slowly from the ceiling, winged with flames. When he looked up, he reeled as the fire snaking out of the door gathered and stood up before him, twisting into an oddly familiar shape. Cinder. Her form flashed, then dulled to the color of smoke. She whined before bounding off to the second door on his left, then leapt up, clawing at it as she keened. "Someone there?" he screamed through the wood, the knob sending a pang of heat through his thick glove. A high cry sailed over the hissing heat. "Get down!" he screamed. He wiped at his mask as Cinder gave him a last look, her dark eyes lit with golden fire before she shifted in the heat, evaporating like a mirage. A scream brought him back to the child behind the door and he sent his axe through until it stuck, yanking the door back with its handle. A little girl lay with her head in her arms as a flameover rolled across the ceiling above her, pushing out a hot wind that knocked him back as her hair lifted in a frenzied halo. When he finally bent to pick her up she was stiff with fear, her terrified face reflected back to her in his mask like a mirror. Her arms circled his neck, squeezing in panic as he ran back through a wall of fire. Edan screamed into his portable, "I've got the girl!"

He could still see her ribbons of hair billow before the yawning flames, dark gold against brilliant light. A warmth on his shoulder startled him back to the reflection in the mirror—a haggard, hollow-eyed man with waves of dark hair falling over his arm as his wife leaned in to kiss his neck. "You okay?" she asked, examining the purple rings around his eyes and the ash-white stubble that dirtied his jaw in their reflection. He fingered her hair, "Yeah," he growled, then cleared his throat. "It's been a hell of a season. Too warm for fall, and dry. Malfunctioning fireplaces and out of control leaf burnings. And Darra … I'm glad you're home, Wyn."

She nodded, kneading his shoulders. "You need a break, Babe. Maybe we should both take some time off. I never knew Darra was into imaginary friends. And a dog?"

He dumped another bag of bite-sized snickers into the neon orange bowl and glanced up, grinning, as Darra skipped into the kitchen. "Daddy, look at me!"

"You look beautiful, Baby." He stooped to kiss her head.

"Do you like my wings? And look, Cinderella's coming too!" She held up her end of the leash for him to see. Edan followed his wife's gaze to the other end, raised up and encircling air as if starch-stiffened. It wobbled about a little and he watched for Wyn's surprise. She only laughed. "A fairy princess and a ghost dog, what a combo! Where'd you find the trick leash, Edan?"

He raised his eyebrows, shrugging. "I found it …"

"Huh. Well, we'll be home soon. Don't forget to switch on the stereo. The ghoulish tunes are set to go."

"Yeah, I always like to see the little monsters boogie," he smirked, straightening Darra's tiara. "Be safe."

Later that night Darra sank to the floor, her glittering gown puffing up around her, pink lip gloss smudged across one cheek. She spread the pile, scanning for sweet tarts. "How'd it go?" Edan wondered.

Wyn smiled over their daughter, her eyes shining with a combination of affection and concern. "She could have won an Oscar tonight. Everyone kept commenting on how she played up her imaginary dog by petting it and talking to it. An older woman over on Radcliff asked if she was Cinderella but Darra told her she was the Fairy Godmother and the dog was Cinderella." She looked up at him, her eyes glistening as she whispered, "I'm a little concerned, Edan. She hasn't stopped talking about 'Cinderella' since I came home. Should we be worried about this?"

"I might have started it." Edan reddened under his wife's glare, "I … we were just playing." His voice fell away as he stared into the hazel eyes that sought his attention, a lolling tongue licking the wet nose beneath them. Wyn clutched at his arm, holding back a scream. He held her, stroking her thick hair. "I know," he whispered, "I think I dreamed her. I'm sorry, Wyn. I didn't know how to tell you."

"*What is she?*"

Darra glanced up at the sound of her mother's strained voice. She followed their gaze to Cinder and stroked her all too tangible fur as the dog lay panting beside her. "Can Cinderella have a candy, too?"

"No!" her parents croaked together.

They sat holding each other tightly on the floor just inside Darra's bedroom. Cinder opened one eye, peeking at them from her spot on the foot of the little girl's bed. Her tail thumped softly before she settled back to sleep. "I thought you'd made the whole thing up, just to indulge her," Wyn whispered, "Where did she come from?"

"I don't know. I mean I carried her out of that house on Oak. Wyn, I'm telling you, she was *dead*! She had no pulse, she was totally limp in my arms. She was cold, for God's sake!"

"And you offered to bury her in our yard?"

"I just felt sorry for her. The only person who loved her was gone and I just wanted to give her a good resting place. I was carrying her back to the station and she just … jumped out of my arms. God, Wyn, I don't know. I was exhausted. I don't know what I saw."

"But Darra saw her."

"Yeah, that's the thing. She always saw her. Even when Mrs. Byrd came over and acted like she was still dead, like nothing was there … Even when I couldn't see her. But I heard her, whining at the door later that night, and there she was again."

"And then I came home."

"And she was gone again, Wyn! What the hell was I supposed to say?"

She shrugged, snuggling deeper into his embrace. "Darra believed in her. That's why she always saw her. You were cynical; I was oblivious. Mrs. Byrd was convinced."

"I saw her in the fire," he breathed. Wyn searched his eyes. "She led me to that little girl." He wept, then; spilling the burden of their daughter's well being and the blazing despair that burned through his memories. It seemed as though his every thought was blackened with the same wet char they left after a fire.

Wyn pressed her warm fingers over his wet face. "She's here *now*, Edan. Maybe it's like a fairy tale. You just have to believe."

THE HAUNTS OF ALBERT EINSTEIN
Larry Hodges

For every living human being in the world today, there are about thirty from the past who, by virtue of no longer being alive, are now dead. So while there are about 6.6 billion living humans on the planet, there are about 200 billion dead humans.

Ghosts.

Now ghosts don't want to be dead just anywhere. Would you want to be dead for eternity in some desolate ocean covered with plankton? Or freezing your ectoplasm off on some desolate glacier with a bunch of dancing penguins? Or, God help you, in *New Jersey*? So there are only about 22 million square miles of land that are deadable for ghosts.

That's 9000 ghosts per square mile. *Nine Thousand!* If you think Earth is crowded with humans with their paltry 300 per square mile, imagine what it's like for the 9000 ghosts. *Sardines!*

That's why the ghost of Albert Einstein, no longer constrained by the artificial ethical concerns created by the prefrontal cortex of a living human brain, decided to solve the problem of ghost proliferation. There were just too many ghosts—relatively speaking—and Einstein felt crowded by all the ghostly bodies.

He rested his non-corporeal head on his non-corporeal hand, deep in thought as he floated about in his old office at the Institute for Advanced Study at Princeton which, he suddenly realized, was in New Jersey. A shiver ran down his ghostly spine.

Several dozen ghosts floated about in the small office, some of them heatedly arguing physics. Einstein was sick of these arguments, but what could he do? They were all jammed together, inmates in the hereafter. Einstein wasn't sure what was worse, the constant bickering from his colleagues, or the deafening stench of the Neanderthal ghosts. "If they would just take an occasional shower!" he thought.

Worse, the hated paparazzi ghosts had recently found him, making his death a living hell. Even now, he could imagine them outside with their ghostly cameras, searching for him, always searching, searching, hoping to get another picture of him with his hair unkept or his tongue stuck out and plastering it on posters and shirts everywhere. Einstein shook his head. Could death get any worse?

A living physicist named Dr. Smith sat at Einstein's old desk, scribbling notes, unaware of his ghostly companions. Light reflected off his bald head and off a glittering yellow diamond he wore on a ring. Einstein floated over to Smith and, looking over the man's shoulder at his notes, smirked. "I figured that out when I was thirteen," he said to the oblivious Smith.

Several nearby ghosts giggled. Back when he was alive, Einstein had made the mistake of collecting artifacts from famous physicists, astronomers and other celebrities, and many of these artifacts were still in his old office. It wasn't until he too was dead that he learned their past owners haunted many of these artifacts.

Einstein turned to these past owners. "Let's face it, guys, there simply isn't enough room on this planet for two hundred billion ghosts."

"We could relocate to Mars," said Percival Lowell. "The Martians will welcome us." Lowell saw the skeptical stares from the other ghosts. "I've seen them! *Really!*"

"Sure, Percy," said Galileo, shaking his head. "Have you ever tried looking through a modern telescope?"

"We can't go to Mars anyway," said Harry Houdini, the only non-scientist in the room other than the smelly Neanderthals. "We're ghosts, doomed to haunt this planet forever." He threw up his hands. "We'll never escape."

"I have an idea," said Robert Oppenheimer. "Why don't we try blowing the excess ghosts off the planet with those nuclear bombs we found hidden in Iraq?"

Many of the ghosts in the room grabbed Oppenheimer and pitched the yelping scientist against the wall. They knew that ghosts that stick together, stay dead together.

"Let's try to solve the problem with a thought experiment," Einstein suggested.

"I'm sick and tired of your thought experiments," replied Erwin Schrödinger. "We always end up with dead cats."

Werner Heisenberg looked up. "And we never really know if the cats are dead or alive."

Isaac Newton was shaking his head. "This just shows the supremacy of Newtonian Physics," he said as he elbowed Gottfried Leibniz in the ribs. The two got into a loud shoving contest while Schrödinger began to wail about dead cats.

"Can you guys please shut up?" asked the mechanical voice of Stephen Hawking, who was visiting from Cambridge. "Even I can hear you, and I'm still mostly alive." He rolled his wheelchair behind the desk next to Dr. Smith, and looked over his notes. Hawking smirked. "I figured all that out when I was eleven," he told the embarrassed Smith. "Albert, you said you didn't get all this until you were *thirteen*?"

Einstein glared at Hawking. Einstein had spent years cultivating his image with his wild hair and tales of his exploits in Nazi Germany. And then along came this young whipper-snapper stuck in a wheelchair and talking through a voice synthesizer, and so everyone felt sorry for him. *Well, whoopee do!* Einstein had won the Nobel Prize and was *Time Magazine's* "Man of the Century," and yet who got all the press these days? It just wasn't fair.

Realizing that he'd get no help from his irritating colleagues and wondering if Oppenheimer's idea of blowing them all off the planet wasn't such a bad idea, Einstein went to work on his own. He floated back and forth, deep in thought, trying to ignore the bickering, the Neanderthal stench, and whenever he passed the window, the flashes from the paparazzi cameras.

Einstein gave a ghostly smile as he solved the problem. He was good at thinking outside the box. Or in this case, thinking inside the sphere.

In theory, causing the sun to explode was relatively simple. You just increase this do-dad in the equation so that it's greater than the thingamajiggy there, balance the equation, set the squiggly thing to infinite, and solve for alpha. In practice, it meant building a doomsday device.

He fetched the still-sulking Robert Oppenheimer and the other ghosts from the old Manhattan Project, explained the problem, and presto! Two months later, they sent their creation into the sun, and it went *Bang!*, utterly obliterating the Earth and humanity, and adding 6.6 billion new ghosts to the bursting mass of ghostanity.

Einstein had figured that with Earth gone, the ghosts would now haunt that region of space the planet once occupied. Since Earth's volume had been 260 billion cubic miles, that would be over a cubic mile for every ghost.

The thought had brought a smile to Einstein's lips. A cubic mile, all to himself! No more bickering physicists, or babbling about dead cats, or the disgusting Neanderthal stench. Even the hated paparazzi ghosts would have trouble finding him in 260 billion cubic miles!

But Einstein was a physicist, not a spiritualist, or he might have realized that ghosts are bound to things, not places. Move a haunted house, and the ghost doesn't haunt the vacant lot; it haunts the haunted house, wherever it might be. Burn down the house, and it haunts whatever bits of it remain.

The only thing nearby that had survived the rather sudden and extreme global warming was the glittering yellow diamond from Dr. Smith's finger. Einstein, still full-sized, found himself bound to the glittering diamond as it shot off into the far reaches of space. Suddenly he greatly missed New Jersey. Things *are* relative, he realized.

But Einstein was not alone. The other nearby ghosts, dozens of them, were also bound to the diamond, their legs and feet squished together into one ethereal mass on the tiny diamond. Their squirming and translucent bodies stuck out in all directions, like an otherworldly sea urchin. Newton, Leibniz and the other physicists were bickering, Schrödinger babbled about dead cats, Houdini wailed about being stuck again, and the Neanderthals continued to smell. And it didn't take long before the paparazzi ghosts, also bound to the diamond, were flashing their cameras in Einstein's face, as they would for the rest of eternity.

SAFE UPON THE SHORE
Kou K. Nelson

———◆———

I kept watch on the cliff's edge at the turning of the tide, just as my mistress bade me for the past ten years.

"For what am I looking?" I asks that first day, knowing no better as a Newfoundlander girl but of a dozen years.

"A sign," says she.

"What kind of a sign?"

"You'll knows when you sees it," she says and cuffed me for asking.

So, I went to the cliff's edge, waiting and looking. I tells her about the single gull and she says that weren't a sign nor was the minke whale that ventured into Harbour Deep a month too early for migration.

"No," says she, "it'll be a sign you'll not mistake."

And so I continued watching, day after day, searching the horizon and the shore, looking for anything what might be a sign. I watched these long ten years, and never did I see anything that my mistress found to be a sign.

Today, there was naught but white as gauzy as a bride's veil. The coast was hemmed in and I cursed my mistress for making me stand in the cold damp, the wind lashing my face with my hair, skirt and apron snapping like a banner.

"I'm like to fly off the cliff as much as fall," says I, straining my eyes to see more than a foot ahead.

The Labrador Sea roared before me, so the edge was close, but I would get such a beating if I came home too soon. And then the fog lifted and I saw the usual rocky strand strewn with spume as the tide pulled away.

"What's that?" I says, lifting a hand to my brow to cut the glare. "Seals come ashore?" I counted the cluster of black figures laid out on a stretch of sand, the wisps of fog making it hard to decipher much more. *One, two, three ... fourteen!*

A small figure ran towards them, and by the skipping gait, I knew it to be wee Denny White.

"Denny!" calls I, taking care to not let my voice get lost in the wind. "Is them seals?" The figures stirred, and I knew they were not. The sign! "Denny! Tell Father Forthswaite to ring the bells! Tell him to ring them now!"

Denny slowed his pace, wavering between the shadows on the beach and my command.

"Denny," says I, mustering the most threatening tone I could muster. "You'll go to Father Forthswaite or I'll box your ears and tell your ma that you didn't hearken!"

And so he ran towards the church as I hurried towards my mistress and the house. The sign! I was sure this was the sign of which she spoke. I ran as I'd never run before, tripping on the skirts wrapped about my legs, but I rose as quickly as I fell. She had promised me a sign what could not be mistaken and here it was now clear as the day became. *Fourteen, as many as were lost on the* Theresa Maria, *those dozen years back!*

My mistress must've seen me coming as she met me in the yard, drawing aside the laundry on the line.

"What is it?" says she, although by the light in her worried face she knew well enough. "What is it you've seen, Maggie?"

I'd used most of my breath for the running and could hardly gasp as the wind stole any further breath away.

"It's them, mistress," I says. "It's them! They've come home!"

She looked at me with wild eyes, her mouth gaping as if the wind stole her breath as well. The church bells split the silence and I was proud of Denny for doing as he was bid for once.

"They're home," she says, falling instantly still, her worry lifting on the air and leaving as she gazed over my shoulder to the sea beyond. "My Ned has come home."

My feet itched as I awaited her wish.

Her weathered hands touched her hair then her face. "I must look a fright," says she. She held out her skirts as if they were another's woman's clothes. "My Ned can't see me like this. He'd hardly recognize me." She frowned then gripped my shoulders. "You'll make his favorite dish, Maggie, brewis with scrunchions, and a bakeapple crumble."

"Yes, ma'm." Though no sailor I knew wanted hard tack and salt cod as a welcome home. Then again, we weren't expecting any ordinary sailor.

"Better a jigg's dinner," says she, as if hearing my thoughts. "Toutons, for sure, with a good dollop of molasses."

"Yes, ma'm."

"And put the kettle on."

"Yes, ma'm"

She looked past the house. "He'll be here soon." She furrowed her brow and gave a hard nod. "Best get to cooking, maid."

"Yes, ma'm." I curtsied before she could ask for more and hurried back to the house with her close on my heels.

Never had the old woman climbed stairs with such vigor!

The pots and pans rattled in my hands but it were no use trying to quiet them. Who knew what to expect at the door? Twelve years was a long time at sea, and surely longer without a boat, as the wreckage had long arrived without its crew.

I reminded myself that thirteen other homes were doing the same as we, including Denny White's. It weren't from cruelty that I stopped him from seeing his da. I just thought it best if he met him for the first time with his ma.

The cabbage had just started to boiling when footsteps shuffled outside.

"That'd be him," says my mistress, coming off the stairs, smoothing the front of a dress I'd not seen before, her hair done up as it might have been when she was no more than a girl herself.

She gazed at the shadow on the lace curtain, her eyes matching the blue of her gown. Her hair had grown gray and wiry over the years, her cheeks turned jowly.

"Sure it's your welcoming face he'll want to see first," I says, standing firm before the glowing stove.

"And so he will," says she, but I caught the sharp look she cast my way.

I didn't mind. I was in no hurry to see what awaited.

"Welcome home, Ned!" she called and threw open the door wider than she had for anyone else.

She beamed at the figure before her. I kept my place, not wanting to see the fearsome thing any sooner than need be. She embraced the captain and drew him in, paying no mind to the wetness on him.

As a child I'd seen the captain many times. He was different now, twelve years spent under water. His dark beard and hair glistened starkly against skin thin and pale as a fish's belly. His eyes, the milky cast of sea glass, showed a spark of recognition at the sight of his wife.

"Annie," he sighed, water splashing from his lips as he spoke.

She seemed not to mind the captain's state, caring only that her husband had returned at last. They clung to each other a long while, my mistress' dress turning dark where they touched. They parted awkwardly, as if reminded of my presence.

"And you'll know Maggie Doyle," my mistress says, turning the captain to me. "Sean Doyle's girl."

"Maggie," he says with a gurgle and an extended hand. "You're a grown woman now."

"So it seems, sir." Not wanting to aggravate the spirit, I stepped forward to take his hand and tried to hide my shudder at the chill and slime.

"Come in! Come in, my Ned! My Captain Dearest!" My mistress threaded her arm through his and brought him to the table. "Would a cuppa tea do you? Or perhaps a hot bath to warm your bones?" she offered, only the slightest quake in her tone to show that she spoke to a ghost and not a man.

The captain smiled with teeth smooth as pearls. "I've enough liquid refreshment, thank ye, Annie."

I stifled a laugh, gladdened that the dead kept a sense of humor. My mistress gripped the back of the chair where he once sat.

"But you'll have a bite, won't you, Ned?" She glanced my way. "Maggie's made you a good jigg's dinner."

"And toutons," I added, wanting only to please the spirit who seemed to grow less fearsome by the minute.

He smiled wanly, perhaps at the distant memory of the fine dish.

"Course it won't be as good as your ma's ..." my mistress apologized as she ran a hand through her scraggling hair.

He shrugged. "I can't stay long, Annie," says he, casting her a wistful eye, water dripping from his chin.

"No?" she asks, and the little youth that bloomed in her face was gone.

"The tide'll turn, and I'll be off with it."

My mistress stopped the trembling of her lip by pulling the corners of her mouth tight. "Don't think I'll let you pass so easily, Ned," says she, "It's been twelve long years and I want my due."

He didn't argue with her, but whether because he knew better and there was no point, or because he was agreeing with her, I didn't know. I pulled the plates from the shelf.

The church bells rang again and the captain grinned.

"That would be Shave O'Riordon's doing," says he. "I thought it best if we had a dance at the hall with the rest of the town. I'll be wanting to know what they've been at."

"The hall?"

My heart broke for my mistress as I knew she wanted the captain for herself, especially as he would only walk this earth a short while. Her shoulders drooped, but he would have none of it.

"Grab your shawl, woman," he ordered her lightly. "And, Maggie either put the pot aside or take it with you. Whatever you see fit."

There was no point in letting good food or my hard labor go to waste, so even if the captain didn't want it, there'd be someone at the hall who would. I wrapped the supper in a basket and grabbed my shawl. I set to the streets, joining the throngs heading towards the church to welcome our b'ys home.

It was a wondrous thing, to see the town united as such. The church hall was full to brimming, with all of Harbour Deep present. The widows of the *Theresa Maria's* crew walked gaily alongside their pale sodden men. There was Nell Rogers clinging to Able's arm, resting her cheek so tightly to his shoulder that water wrung from his oil skin coat, and Abby White paid no mind to Murray's bloated face as she dotted it with kisses. And then there was wee Denny White, done as duty called, his head held so high, he was near as tall as his ma. He swung from his da's hand, the slip and slime giving him no pause.

I set my basket to the table, alongside all the others. The trestle groaned and creaked under the burden. The living set to eating while the dead looked on and rekindled old acquaintances. And then a deep thundering like the pounding of our communal hearts was heard. Jack Peddle answered Billy Hinks' bodhran with the keening of his fiddle. Tom White's whistle began a familiar tune and a great cheer rose. The crowd, young and old, quick and dead, broke longways, men and b'ys to one side, women and maids to t'other. The church floor bowed and thudded with two hundred stomping feet. Hands held and skirts a-whipping, we wove and spun our way through lancers and reels, sharing smiles and greetings, reliving the merry days before the *Theresa Maria* sank.

And too soon the music abruptly stopped.

We held our breaths and looked to our loved ones. The crew looked to their captain.

"She's calling us, b'ys," says he, cocking his head and looking beyond the church walls towards the sea. "It's time."

"Not so soon," my mistress insisted, her fingers pressed deep into the arms of the captain's coat. "You've only just returned."

The captain's brow furrowed as he surveyed the waiting faces of his men. "It's not for me to decide, Annie. She's beckoning and we must obey."

A shriek shrill as any banshee rose from the widows of the *Theresa Maria*. The rest of us joined in their dismay. I had yet to speak with my uncle Jimmy Pollack, and Molly Dowd only just danced with her cousin Bill. There were others with similar pleas until finally, my mistress spoke above the rest.

"We haven't done the Running of the Goat," says she. "You won't leave before we Run the Goat. You'll not break tradition."

The sailors glanced about, worry in their frosty sea glass eyes, though not a one released his widow's hand.

"Just one dance, Ned," my mistress pled. "We always finish with the Running of the Goat. Surely, you won't deprive us of that?"

The captain was wary, but he also did not relinquish his widow's grip. He addressed the whole of the hall, "We'll do the dance, Annie, but know that we can't disobey her. We're a part of the sea as much as the sea is a part of us." As if for emphasis, an extra spray of water flowed from his lips.

"I know, Ned," she assured him, "but we'll have our last dance before I'll let her have you back."

With a sad reluctance, the captain gave a nod and Billy set to drumming and the fiddle and whistle soon joined in, but there was a glint in my mistress' eye that said she would not surrender so easily. The captain's dragging step said the sea wouldn't either.

We stomped and cheered and whooped all the louder as we danced to the rhythm of the goat. We clasped hands then changed partners and when we formed a ladies' chain, a whisper spread, "We'll not let go. We won't let the sea have them back."

When the dance should have ended, the musicians played on, and we easily restarted the steps.

"We must go," the captain says, a tone of worry rising in his voice.

"We must go," his crew echoed, although they continued through the dance as if possessed.

The sailors passed swiftly from one hand to another, none of the women folk letting go until sure the next woman held firm. The music grew in pitch and tempo.

"If the sea wants you," my mistress says, "she'll must come and get you."

At this the captain's milky eyes widened with fear and pity. "And so she shall," says he. "So she shall."

At that he let out a laugh that shook the very timbers of the hall. "She's coming b'ys," he called, then began to choke. "She comes!" Water that once oozed from his lips, now flowed like a cataract with no end.

The men of the *Theresa Maria* writhed and twisted like the catch they had hauled aboard all those years ago, but their widows held fast. The sailors let out a mighty roar and from their mouths sprung tributaries to their captain's river. The church bells tolled, but the widows held fast and the dance continued, a hundred feet splashing on the floor, flouting the call of the sea.

"We'll soon drown," says I, careful not to slip on the churning foam beneath me.

There was no end to the water that flowed from the dead sailors' lips! I slogged forward, struggling to keep my footing. And yet my mistress and the other widows danced all the merrier, growing light as lilies, as the water rose to our knees.

"We must go," says Darryl Hallet, taking my hand and leading me away from the line. "Let us go," says he to any that would hearken.

The young folk took heed, begging the ancients to leave the hall with them. But it was of no use. The widows of the *Theresa Maria* had waited too long for this day and would not leave their loved ones' sides. The water lapped at our waists, and we pushed the children before us.

"To the hill," Nancy Brown called, carrying her sisters in her arms.

"To high ground," those leaving agreed, a child in each hand.

I glanced about and saw Denny White had not gone with the rest.

"Denny," I shouted, seeing that he clung sputtering to the hem of his father's coat. "Come with us, b'y, we'll see to you!"

But Denny wouldn't part from his recently discovered da, though his da seemed to care not a whit, lost in his widow's gaze as the music grew ever more feverish.

"It's not your time, b'y," says I, the water at my chin, my skirts weighing me down while the dancers grew ever more spry.

I wrapped an arm about Denny's middle and pulled with all my might, but the sea was a greedy thing and would not surrender easily. I pulled and kicked, slipping and choking, but I refused to let the sea have what wasn't her due.

The water closed over my head and tumbled me hard with all its force. I held my breath and shut my eyes tight. When I opened them again, all was under water though the lanterns remained lit and the musicians played on. The captain and his crew continued to dance with their widows, their clothing and feet lifting lightly about them, their faces pale and young in the faint green sea light.

Denny White, a blank stare in his eyes, drifted limply among them, a specter among specters, his hair catching the current, waving like kelp. I swam to his side, took hold of his wrist and dodging the widows and their men, brought us both to the door. I passed through expecting cool air, but discovered that while the crew of the *Theresa Maria* claimed the church, the tides had claimed the streets. A faint shadow loomed ahead and I swam towards it. I finally broke the surface, gasping for air.

"Take hold, maid," Darryl Hallet beckoned.

I grabbed the rope offered and the b'ys hauled us to land. Alan McCann threw Denny over his shoulder and we all ran to the top of the hill, not daring to glance behind until we could run no further. When we hit dry ground, we set to work on Denny, taking turns thumping and shaking the sea out o' him. At last his blue lips turned pink and we glanced back at Harbour Deep, but by then it was gone, with nothing but a cruel greedy arm of the sea in its place.

"Listen," whispers Molly Dowd.

"What?" says Alan McCann.

"I hear not a thing," says I.

But there it was. We felt more than heard the deep thunder of the bodhran and what we took at first to be reflected moonlight was the water lit by the lanterns from the hall beneath. The dance carried on.

And so must we.

We gathered the children, lit a fire, and built shelter. We sought food and made ourselves warm. The shelters became a village and which soon enough became a town once more. Our b'ys grew to be men with young b'ys of their own and they followed in the ancients' footsteps, making their living from the sea, and paying her their respects. Except for Denny White.

On nights when the moon is dark, we know where to find old Denny White. He's gone to the harbor once more to look for his ma and da, his head cocked, listening for drumming of the bodhran, his rheumy eyes studying the water for dancing lantern light. We know he's waiting for a sign. What kind, we aren't sure, but we have no doubt, he'll knows it when he sees it. And when he does, he'll alert us again, and for him, we'll Run the Goat once more.

WENDIGO
Shannon Robinson

———————◆———————

Clifford didn't call that often, but when he did call, he'd be drunk. Drunk, or well on the way to being drunk. He never called our older sister, and he didn't call our mother or our father at their separate homes. Just me.

He was drunk the last time I spoke with him—two weeks before his death. Six months ago. He called from his apartment in Berlin, where he'd been living for the past ten years, a self-exiled Boho. He wanted to reminisce about our childhood, to talk about when we'd gone to see the opening of *Star Wars*, what an event that had been. How we'd both been barely old enough to read the scrawl (*A long time ago, in a galaxy far, far away…*) but knew it was going to be our religion. How our fat British cousin had been our reluctant chaperone. How after all the hype, *The Phantom Menace* sucked, and George Lucas was a traitor and an ass. Clifford didn't remember that he'd talked to me about this the last time he called, rehashing the same details, working himself up into the same rant through which I had to shout to communicate that I agreed with him, agreed about everything. I had loads of work to do—a stack of manuscripts from the slush pile to write reports on—but I didn't want to rush Clifford off the phone. His girlfriend, Taina, had gone to sleep, leaving him to keep drinking alone; she had to work in the morning. He promised to mail me a CD of the song he was working on. I didn't think he would, but I looked forward to it, despite myself. And then he had that car crash, drunk driving, no surprise. Except it was a surprise. Lost

42

lamb, black sheep: I hadn't thought he'd just disappear one day.

Fall in Toronto brings with it long, chilly evenings. I was at home, half watching some black-and-white movie on television, half reading a manuscript about a ritual abuse survivor. If I could just commit to the movie, I'd enjoy it; if I could just focus on the book, I'd finish my work. But I sat on the floor in front of the couch, not letting myself get too comfortable. The hour passed eleven, and I could feel a damp draft leaking in through my poorly insulated windows, from the narrow gap under the front door. Cold wind rattled through the trees and shook leaves onto the porch. I didn't turn up the thermostat. I could barely afford rent on my ground-floor urban shanty, never mind heat.

When phone rang, I wondered who would be calling so late at night. No call display to help me—the cheapie handset was just one step up from a rotary dial. I answered on the third ring. "Hello?" I said, with an edge of accusation.

"Hah-lo," said the voice on the other end of the line.

A door opened in my head. My lips parted, but I couldn't speak.

"Hello? Can you hear me?" the caller said. He sounded impatient, and a little drunk.

"Hello? Who is this?"

"S'me."

"I'm sorry—who?"

"It's your eld-er broth-er." He drew out the syllables, enunciating like a cartoon aristocrat.

"Yeah, you've got the wrong number."

"Maggie, ferfuck's sake. It's me!"

"Look, I don't know who you are. But this isn't funny. It's sick. Don't call here."

I hung up and then unplugged the phone. I even took the receiver off the cradle, which made no sense, but it made me feel better. The two halves of the phone sat side by side on my coffee table, joined by the umbilical smile of the cord, the black plastic casing smudged with fingerprints. The caller must have been someone who knew Clifford, some enemy, some weird friend. Maybe that buddy of his who used to tape prank calls—he could be recording my outraged reaction for a performance piece. Getting off on it. I didn't want to think about it. It was like the time I saw an old man masturbating on the subway, or the time I saw a dying cat twisting in the gutter, coated with spray paint. Nothing you wanted to linger over.

The next late-night call to my apartment came within a few weeks, as

I was plowing through a true-crime manuscript that mapped Canadian serial killers' activities over the last century.

"Hah-lo." The voice made me pull the receiver from my ear.

"Hey, asshole—"

"Mmmyes, I'm an asshole. Your brother is an asshole. Woof-woof-woof." That's what Clifford always said, in place of *blah, blah, blah.* "Taking that as read—"

"Where are you calling from?"

"From our flat. I'm sitting out on the loggia." During Clifford's years abroad, certain eccentric turns of phrase had taken up residence in his vocabulary.

"What do you want?"

There was a pause, and I could hear the faint swish of liquid. "I want Taina to marry me. I just can't make her happy. I just can't. I ask her to marry me, and she says she won't." Clifford had said this to me before, almost those exact words, more than once. And the familiar monologue continued: Taina didn't believe in marriage, and there was no common-law in Germany. His solution, he said, was to sleep around. His solution was not to tell her or leave her. He loved and respected her.

"Enough. Enough, enough, enough," I said over top of the words pouring from the receiver, and I hung up.

Before unplugging the phone, I dialed the code for call return. I got an automated message stating that the number could not be traced. I found Clifford's number in an old address book that I kept shelved with my college yearbooks. After I punched in the long string of digits, a recorded voice said,

Kein Anschluss unter dieser Nummer. Dies ist eine Aufzeichnung.

Of course that number was disconnected. Taina had also been killed in the car crash. Served her right for letting Clifford drive drunk. For letting him be drunk, for so long.

The next day, I phoned my sister, Kristen, in Ottawa. I waited till after dinner, when I knew she'd be more relaxed. She'd been a television producer before she was a stay-at-home mom, and had never quite left that intensity behind. Her usual speaking voice always hovered near top volume; her efficiency sometimes bordered on impatience.

"I need you to believe me when I tell you this," I said.

"Okay. Hang on a sec—ZACHARY! COME BACK AND CLOSE THE SCREEN DOOR PROPERLY!—Go on."

"I think Clifford's been calling me."

Someone was imitating Clifford, Kristen said. Or I was dreaming it all. No, I told her, it seemed so real.

"What have you been taking?" she asked.

"Nothing. Xanax."

"Maybe you're having a flashback."

"From what? I've never done any of that kind of crap." This was a family trait: we were all snobbish about the particular drugs we didn't take.

It was a con, Kristen insisted.

"Next time he calls," she said, "just hang up right away. It's not him, all right? Clifford's gone."

It wasn't that my sister didn't believe in ghosts, too. We were raised by the same superstitious Catholic mother, after all. It was that Clifford had become an abstract for her, long ago. He was a fact, a photographic negative, a puzzle piece in the kitchen junk drawer—a portion of some lost, larger whole, never to be assembled. About two years ago, she'd told him, "Don't call me when you've been drinking."

And so he stopped calling her.

I was lying in bed with my disc player on the pillow beside me, listening to the last song Clifford had sent me. I wanted to hear his voice, his actual voice, for purposes of comparison.

You lay me down like a broken road
I need another hit of the marigold
These days have the feel that nothing is real
I wake up beside you alone

I liked the song, but at the same time, I couldn't tell if it was any good. Clifford had moved to Berlin because he'd had some dream of making it big on the European music scene—like the Beatles, who started out playing in dives in Hamburg. So much for that. I tried writing out the lyrics to the song and reading them dispassionately, but I could hear his voice singing them, in my head. He would sing in a kind of hush, in a voice slightly hoarse with cigarettes.

I used to have this one cassette tape he'd made of his music—not a studio recording, just him and his acoustic. You could hear traffic behind him, a soft whoosh of tires on pavement and the squeak of his fingers on the guitar strings. I loved that tape. But somehow it got lost in one of my moves from one apartment to another. I'd have nothing to play it on now, anyway.

Talking to my parents about the phone calls was out of the question. Mom would interpret my story as some strange guilt trip about the fact that instead of having Clifford buried, she'd had him cremated and his ashes stowed in a brass urn on a mausoleum shelf in Ottawa. His first trip home in ten years. There had been no funeral. Despite commandeering the logistics, my mother had insisted on being defensive about the arrangements. I was just relieved that his remains had been taken care of. Both my paternal grandparents' ashes had gotten "lost" in our basement for years before being properly interred. As for my father, I knew he was unable to talk about anything that strayed into the realm of feelings and the nonrational. He tended to generate a peculiar quality of silence—one that presented modest but somehow impenetrable barriers. This is how I imagined our conversation would go:

Me: Dad, have you heard from Clifford?

Dad: *****

Me: Because someone's been calling me, pretending to be him.

Dad: *****

Me: But really, I think it's him.

Dad: *****

He would just evaporate like that, even if you were sitting with him face to face.

Over the years, Clifford had only ever called at the worst times: when I was running out the door, when I was busy, when I was exhausted. A week or so after I'd spoken to Kristen, I was working on an overdue report when the phone rang.

"Hah-lo."

I drew in a breath. "Clifford?"

"I also answer to 'Genius' and 'Love God.' But you may call me 'Pongo.'" He laughed, and said he'd just got back from playing a gig.

"What time is it there?"

"Dunno. What time is it there?"

"Ten."

"So … four in the morning. Should be getting light soon." He asked whether I ever visited the building Grandma and Grandpa used to live in on Bloor Street, and began to recount all kinds of details of the place as he remembered it—the nailbrush shaped like a seahorse in the bathroom, the coral-colored bedspreads, the earthy smell of our grandfather's pipe.

"Where's Taina? Is she there with you?"

"No, she's on a business trip."

He then began to complain once again about how she was always away on business trips. That he just couldn't make her happy, and she wouldn't marry him even though she'd lived with him for two years. So he slept around. He would never tell her about it or leave her. He loved and respected her. And there was no common-law in Germany.

"I need to get some rest. You need to get some rest," I said, finally. It took me twenty minutes to wind down the conversation.

"I love you very, very much. You're the most important person in the world to me. You're always in my thoughts, my little sister."

That's what Clifford would always say at the end of his phone calls—an extravagant outpouring of affection. It would have bordered on the theatrical if he weren't slurring. I told him I loved him too, and got off the phone. As I sat on the couch, my hand rested against the receiver for a moment, pressing it down. The black plastic felt warm.

Clifford continued to call. He wanted to talk about growing up in Ottawa—toys we'd played with, places we'd visited, adults who'd scared us. Sometimes he would cry. Other times, he ranted. He couldn't understand our parents' divorce, which had happened while he was away; he thought Dad's infidelities were to be expected. He missed his girlfriend. He missed me. He mixed up my name with Taina's. Sometimes, he'd be only a little tipsy at the beginning of the call, but he would keep drinking while we talked and end up tanked, the booze pushing his consonants into clumsy familiarity with one another. He said all the great artists drank, and he quoted Dylan Thomas's famous last words: "I've had eighteen straight whiskeys. I think that's the record." Then he laughed until he had a coughing fit.

Talking with Clifford reminded me of a series of story-time records I owned as a child: you played the record, and at various intervals you were supposed to read out particular responses from a booklet. You could say whatever you liked, but of course the records would always tell the same tales, follow the same dark grooves. I began to feel dread every time the phone rang, yet I couldn't bring myself to unplug it. I even started to recognize that it would be Clifford from the ring, its particular tone. It sounded lower. I'd pick up, every time.

After weeks of this, I set up a lunch date with René, my ex-boyfriend. He'd begun dating a woman who wasn't too keen on me; I knew I should back off, but I needed to talk to someone who wouldn't dismiss me as a nut-job. René used to tell ghost stories in the Cree tradition, passed down from his mother. At one point he'd been working on a catalogue of folkloric creatures with an emphasis on oral anecdotes. Now he was pursuing an MBA.

We met at a bistro near the university. It was getting a bit too cold for the outdoor patio, so we were the only patrons seated in the bare forest of chairs and tables, hunched in our coats, René periodically clutching his wine glass to make sure it didn't fall over in the wind.

"What am I, your shaman?" he said, after listening to me talk.

Don't be a dick, I told him; I just wanted to know what he thought was going on.

"Well, he sounds like a wendigo. A hungry ghost."

"Explain," I said.

René pulled a spiral notebook from his bag and began making a sketch. The figure that took shape from his pen looked like a lean fox, standing upright—bigger than a man, with protruding ribs. René smiled to himself as he shaded the bones.

"A wendigo," he said, "is always ravenous. The more he eats, the bigger he gets, and so the hungrier he gets, the more desperate. Some people say wendigos used to be human. They can shape-shift and they can possess."

I looked at the sketch-in-progress. The creature had sharp, stained teeth.

"I don't think that's who I'm talking to."

"He's feeding off your emotions." Talons lengthened under René's pen-strokes.

"What should I do?"

René stopped drawing and looked up. I thought he was reaching to hold my hand, but he picked up his wine glass instead.

"Stop feeding him, Maggie."

That sounded very sensible, very sane. But if I stopped speaking to Clifford, who else could he talk to?

One night, Clifford was in a belligerent mood and doing his best to bait me. He began by saying wasn't it ironic that he'd quit piano lessons while I carried on dutifully, yet he was the one who turned out to be the musician. And here we were still following the same paths: I was still kowtowing to the rules, while he was breaking them, making art, playing every night to packed bars.

"Clifford, you're dead."

"No, *you're* dead. You're the one who's working for those fucktard publishers, churning out rubbish, celebrity biographies—"

"No, Clifford. You're *dead*. You died in a car crash."

"Ha-ha ha ha ha. Woof-woof-woof."

He moved on to talking about how he'd always looked up to me when we were at school, what a great student I was, so much smarter than those arsehole teachers. Did I remember Mr. Landow, what a *schwanzlutsher* he was?

I was sleeping very badly. Even nights when Clifford didn't call and I finally managed to drift off, I'd dream that the phone was ringing only to wake up to sudden silence. Or I'd dream that Clifford was talking to me on the phone, his speech unspooling and coiling around my head. During the day, I was exhausted—I drank too much coffee, and the caffeine made my taste buds apathetic. I lost weight. People complimented me on it. My boss, however, wanted to know why I was taking so long to turn around manuscripts. She sounded angry at first, then mellowed and reminded me not to get bogged down, to skim for the big picture.

I kept her words in mind as I sat down at my dining room table and began to sort through the papers I'd lugged home from the office. But before I began to work, I felt compelled to have a look at René's wendigo drawing, which I kept tucked in the pages of my agenda: I found myself pulling it out to look at it several times a day. The ink was smudged from when I'd folded it; the animal's features were dark and blurred. Each time I set eyes on the creature, somehow I was taken aback—how ferocious and starved it looked. I pushed the manuscripts aside and pressed the drawing flat on the table. Directly across from me on a bookshelf was a picture of my brother, one I'd framed a month after he died. It wasn't a great picture—he'd obviously taken it himself, and he was scowling into the camera at the end of his outstretched arm—but it was the only recent photo I had of him. His ashy blond hair had faded from light gold over time, just like mine. When we were very young, we used to be mistaken for twins. Same eyes, same coloring, same profiles. Now his complexion looked waxy and coarse, and his eyes disappeared in a squint. I looked again at the wendigo, with its bony limbs and sinister hunch. I pictured the animal in an empty, unlit apartment, crouched on all fours, its jaw open in front of a phone receiver, ropy saliva dropping to the floor. No.

The following day, a Friday, I decided that if Clifford was going to

call me, I'd be ready for him. I had two drinks at the bar across the
street from the publisher's, for once joining the other editorial assistants
in their ritual end-of-week paycheck blowout, and I bought two bottles
of chintzy chardonnay on the way home. Three-quarters of the way
through the first bottle, I thought Clifford might not call. When the
phone rang, I almost dropped it, I was so fumbly-jumbly. All my limbs
felt very soft and warm.

"Hah-lo," he said.

"I'm drunk," I said.

"No, that's my name," he said.

"Then quit talking to yourself," I said.

We laughed and kept on like that, riffing ridiculously. I am a sloppy,
silly drunk, which is one of the reasons I don't drink that often. When I
spoke, it was like stumbling around in the dark, tripping over things. But
it was also like being borne along by rushing water—the conversation
surged and flowed, almost ahead of my thoughts. Whatever we spoke
about, late into the night, felt profound, powerfully intimate.

In the morning, I couldn't really remember anything we'd said. I felt
emptied out. It was as if I were emerging from some chloroformed
stupor, tender and poisoned. The back of my skull throbbed while I lay
in bed, staring at the stucco ceiling. Slowly, I formed a vague plan to
doctor myself with some greasy delivery food. I dragged myself out to
the living room and picked up the phone.

There was someone on the line.

"I'm coming to visit you," the voice said, quietly.

Then the line hummed its dial-tone, one note—perhaps two or three,
a chord—sustaining and growing louder. I hung up. And then ran to the
bathroom to be sick.

I dressed hastily, stuffed some manuscripts into my bag, and headed
out. My hands kept shaking, and I knew it wasn't the hangover or the
cold weather. A coffee clerk smiled at me pityingly as I fumbled with my
change, like I had some affliction. Perhaps I did. While at the library,
despite the cozy leather armchair I settled into, I found it hard to focus
on my work. The memory of that quiet voice kept replaying itself: *I'm
coming to visit you.* It had sounded like Clifford, and yet it sounded …
wrong. Too close somehow, like he'd been speaking through a tube into
my ear. The library was so overheated, the air above the radiators
shimmered. At one point, I caught a whiff of damp dirt—a mustiness, a
scent of decay. I turned to look around me, and realized it was coming
from an old man, dressed in a tattered overcoat, surrounded by stacks of

yellowing note pages.

Night was falling by the time I returned home. I turned on every light, not caring about the utility bill. After I clicked on the lamp by the couch, I hesitated before reaching over to unplug the phone. A small pinch of its clear plastic tab and it was done, its tail amputated. I wanted to feel more comforted by this gesture. I parked myself in front of the TV with a bowl of re-heated noodles, thinking that maybe a few hours of movies would help me fall asleep.

During the second movie, a copy of *Double Indemnity* I'd borrowed from the library, I thought the VCR was making strange noises—a shuffling beat running beneath the swell of the music score. Piece of shit, I thought, and turned it off to inspect the tape.

But the noise was coming from the door, just a few feet to my left. It sounded like scuffling, like a rhythmic scraping against the wood. The sound was at once distinct and completely unreal: a black tear through white silence.

As I crept towards the door, the scraping changed pitch, and became louder and faster. I put my hand on the doorknob—or more like, I watched myself place a hand on the doorknob. Something frantic, aggressive, wanted in. The door began rattling in its frame, the doorknob vibrating against my palm. A whisper, inside my head, said, *it's so cold and dark outside, so lonely*. My heart thumped painfully in my chest, as if it would burst through its cage of bones. I pictured the doorknob rotating on its own, a seam of darkness forming, widening at the edge of the door—

Wrenching myself away sent a flash of pain through my arm like a jolt from an electric current, nauseating and intense. The lamp toppled and smashed when I groped for the phone to plug it back in. With the page ripped from my address book in hand, I dialed my brother's number. This time, someone picked up. Instantly, the scuffling stopped.

"Clifford?" I said.

"Clifford!" I cried.

"I'm coming to visit you," he replied, as if we'd been in the middle of a conversation. "I've booked my flight. It's all arranged. I'll be crossing the ocean."

"That's what you always promised—and I miss you, I've missed you so much—but then it never happened. And now—"

"Yes?"

"It's too late."

"Yes, it's very late, Maggie."

"No, *too* late," I said, my throat tightening.

"Hmm. Should be getting light soon," he said. He began to sing the words to some old song, sweetly.

"Are you all right?" I asked.

"Of course I'm all right. Can't say how I'll feel in the morning."

"Where are you?" I began crying so hard, it was difficult to talk. "God, where are you?"

"Don't you know? I'm out on the loggia."

"But I need you to be here!" I dropped the phone and ran to unlock the door. I flung it open with such force, the knob smashed into the wall.

Nothing was there but the empty porch, overlooking a patch of weeds. I crouched down and wailed to the deserted street. My brother, my real brother, wasn't coming back.

I returned inside to grab up the phone. Wind blew in from the open door and I shouted,

"We aren't doing this anymore."

"I've written you a song," he said, so calm. Everything in me wanted to say, play it for me, play me that song.

"Don't call me when you're drunk," I said, each word painful, like disgorging a stone. "Not ever."

On the other end of the line, I thought I could hear music, some strange, acoustical melody, but it sped up until it became a garble of notes, accompanied by another sound like liquid rushing down a drain. The layered noises became fainter and fainter until there was only silence.

I don't remember hanging up: I just remember looking at the black receiver in its cradle and realizing that I had.

Clifford never called again.

THE LITTLE HOUSE AT BULL RUN CREEK
Robbie MacNiven

The rain began at four. By six, Captain Small knew they could go no farther. The dirt track had been reduced to a cloying quagmire and the whole troop was drenched and dejected, men and horses both. Manassas junction was still nearly five miles distant and visibility was so poor the Union cavalrymen could have been in amongst a rebel patrol before they even knew it.

"There's a house just at the end of the lane," Corporal Perry shouted over the downpour. "Looks deserted!"

"Looks can be deceiving," Small hollered back. The drenching was making his simmering temper flare. This wasn't how a cavalry raid was meant to play out. Not at all.

"This here's Bull Run Creek, sir!" Perry replied. "Hasn't been three months since General Pope was driven from this very spot! The family probably fled during the battle and haven't been back since!"

"Fine then," Small snapped. "Take Blake and ride ahead. The troop will follow in five minutes. We'll stay inside until this damn rain clears, then press on."

"Understood, sir!"

Perry and Blake cantered off down the lane, the hooves of their steeds kicking up fountains of muck. Within moments the rain's veil had closed around them. Small waited the allotted five minutes, brooding. When no sign of alarm came from ahead he waved the rest of his men on.

The house Corporal Perry had first spotted slowly materialized, a melancholy, dark bulk looming out of the sheeting downpour. As they drew closer Small understood his corporal's conclusions about its state of occupation—the gutters were choked with rainwater, and one of the windows had been staved in. A branch from the lonely apple tree which occupied the yard had snapped off and lay broken and twisted in the mud nearby. The gate to the yard hung open, banging slowly backwards and forwards in the wind.

Perry and Blake were waiting just beyond it. The corporal saluted again.

"We tried the front door, sir, but it's locked. No answer from inside. There are stables out back though, enough room for all the horses."

"Good," Small grunted. "Sergeant Cogburn, dismount the troop. We'll stop here for a few hours, see if we can't get the carbines dry. At this rate the powder will be soaked right through."

"Yes, sir."

As the cavalry troop filed into the yard, Small kicked his boots from his stirrups and threw the reigns to Trooper Blake. Then, motioning Perry to follow, he trudged through the muck to the front door. Overhead thunder grumbled, and the captain couldn't help but draw comparisons with the sound of twelve pounders. It was not a comforting similarity. He ducked in under the front porch.

"I tried already," Perry offered as the captain began to knock. Small ignored him. The sound of his rapping reverberated through the house.

Nothing. He knocked again. Again, nothing. He tried the handle. It was locked. Just as he was about to tell Perry to put his shoulder to good use, he finally caught a sound from inside, muffled but audible.

"Just one moment!" called a voice. A man's voice. Perry's wide eyes met his captain's.

"You goddamn idiot! You said this place was deserted!"

"I ..."

"If these people are rebels then what? We'll have to tie them up or take them with us! Hell, they could already have alerted the local garrison! Goddamn it Perry!"

"But I already knocked, Captain," the NCO protested. "There was no answer, I swear!"

"Shut up," Small snapped, focussing on the door. But it remained shut. There were no more noises from inside.

"They're stalling," Small growled. "Take six men and cover the back. If anyone tries to leave, stop them. Do you think you can managed that?"

"Yes, sir."

"Go."

Perry hurried back out into the rain. Small took a breath and, bracing himself, slammed his shoulder into the door.

It gave with a splitting crack, the cavalryman's momentum carrying him clean over the threshold and into the musty darkness within. He stumbled to a halt, hand reaching for the hilt of his sabre, but the gray light filtering in through the broken doorway revealed nothing but a disused, dusty parlor. The noise of the rain thundering off the roof was almost deafening.

Small paused, took a breath, and looked about. Nothing stirred. A staircase lay directly ahead, leading up to a first story landing. The doors left and right were closed. A grandfather clock dominating the wall beside him seemed to have stopped working. There was a mahogany bookcase to his left. Some of the books had fallen and lay scattered across the floor. The rugs underfoot were heavy with dust.

"Hello?" Small called. No response. No sign of whomever had answered his knocking. He turned back to the doorway and shouted out into the yard.

"Troop, on me! I want this entire house searched, top to bottom! Sergeant Cogburn, guard this door! At the double!"

The drenched Union cavalrymen flooded the house, their sabres drawn. Most were happy to just be in out of the wet. Their sopping boots hammered up the staircase and made the floorboards overhead creak. The doors left and right of Small were broken open. One by one, the reports from each room filtered back. All were empty, and seemed to have been for some time.

"There's someone here," Small insisted. "Find him."

But there was nobody. Beds were stripped and looked under, cupboards thrown open, gutted and then smashed, tables overturned, but of the man who had answered Small's knocks there could be found no sign.

"It's a family house," Sergeant Cogburn noted. "A man, his wife and daughter, judging by the clothes. But I don't reckon any living soul's been in here for months."

"Are you implying I'm hearing things, Sergeant?" Small snarled. "Go and see everyone has stabled their horses properly."

"Yes, sir."

Small stalked through to the kitchen and planted himself on a discarded milking stool. He was drenched through. What was more, he dared not order fires to be lit in any of the house's half-dozen grates for fear that the smoke would attract unwanted attention. They were inside enemy territory here. The raid on Manassas Junction was intended to cripple the Confederate supply network in northern Virginia. Small had been overjoyed when his troop had been picked for the job. If only the weather had mirrored his initial elation.

Thunder growled again, closer this time. The rain was still falling. If anything it had gotten worse. The kitchen window was actually rattling under the repeated impacts. Small closed his eyes and leaned back against the wall, trying to ignore the soaking wet and the saddle ache. Five minute's sleep was all he needed. Just a blink and he'd be fighting fit. Perhaps the rain would have lessened off too.

There was blood running down his left leg.

He frowned. Why? Why was there blood running down his leg? Lots of blood, he realized. Staining his light blue pants an ugly shade of black. Pooling in his boot. Expanding silently across the wooden floorboards. He leapt up, crying out in horror.

His eyes snapped open. He was sitting bolt upright, one fist clenching his sword hilt so tightly his knuckles were white. He looked wildly down at his left leg. There was no blood.

Sleep, he realized, leaning back. He must have dozed off. A nightmare, nothing more. He hadn't realized just how tired he was. He scowled. Since when had his imagination been prone to such wild flights of fancy?

It was then, over the sound of the rain's relentless assault, that he heard the cry. It was the sound of a horse in pain. He sat up once more. The sound came again, from outside. The back of the house, he realized. That was where the stables were. What in hell's name was going on? Muttering darkly, the captain stood and headed back out into the deluge.

He reached the stables just in time to witness the horses bolt. Sergeant Cogburn and three others were trying to coax the troop's compliment of mounts into the copious block adjoining the rear of the house. The animals were clearly in distress, unwilling for whatever reason to enter them. Then one broke past Cogburn's grip. It tossed its mane, eyes wide and white with fear, and before the sergeant could get a hand on its bridle, it shot off back down the lane at a frantic gallop.

That was all the incentive the rest of the troop needed. With a chorus of frightened neighs the heavy warhorses barrelled out through Cogburn's cordon, throwing the startled troopers to the mud. Cogburn himself barely managed to avoid being trampled to a pulp by the thundering surge of iron-shod hooves. Small could only roar in impotent rage as he watched every last one of his troop's mounts, his own included, gallop away into the rain.

"What are you doing?" he screamed at Cogburn, hauling the mud-caked NCO to his feet. "What in the name of God? Do you realize what you've just done?"

"I ... they were spooked, sir," Cogburn stammered. He was shaking, whether from cold, the rain, his close escape, or Small's wrath it was unclear. "I've ... I've never seen any of the animals behave like that before. It was like there was something in the stables that frightened them, sir. Like they didn't want to be anywhere near the house!"

Small struck his sergeant across the jaw, hard. The NCO was left sprawling in the mud for a second time.

"Get this incompetent bastard out of my sight," the captain spat at the other troopers. "You've just cost us this entire operation. No horses, no raid. Everyone inside until I figure out what the hell we're meant to do now."

"He was in the kitchen last I saw," Trooper Baker replied. "Think he wants to catch some shut-eye."

Perry nodded his thanks. Waking the irascible captain was probably not a good idea, but then again neither was failing to report for duty once he found himself at a loose end. Sighing inwardly, the corporal made his way down the corridor into the kitchen.

And came up short.

Of Captain Small there was no sign. Indeed, there was not a single member of the troop in sight. But there was a man occupying the room.

He could have been unconscious, or he could have been dead. The mangled wreck that had once been his left leg seemed to indicate the latter. He was laid out on the kitchen table, his eyes closed, his skin an unhealthy shade of white. The blood from his torn limb had stained the woodwork and was slowly pooling on the floor below.

He was wearing a uniform. Even through the fresh plastering of mud and rain, Perry could tell that it was gray.

The corporal backed hastily out, looking for someone, anyone. Where the hell had everyone gone? Where was Baker? He'd been right behind him, hadn't he? The sound of the rain's endless pounding stoked an unreasoning panic in the corporal. Why had nobody reported that there was a rebel on the kitchen table?

"Captain Small?" he called, starting to head back through the house. "Captain?" His voice became increasingly more frantic, his pace picking up until he was dashing from room to room. "Captain Small? Captain Small?"

He burst from the back door just in time to collide with Small. The officer recoiled angrily.

"Watch where you're going, Corporal!"

"Sorry sir, sorry," Perry stammered. "But … there's a rebel in the kitchen, sir …"

"What?" Small demanded, clearly in no mood for games. "What the damn hell are you talking about, Corporal?"

"There's a wounded rebel on the kitchen table, sir. I think he's unconscious. He could be dead."

"Don't be such an idiot, Corporal. I was in there not five minutes ago. Alone."

"He's there right now, sir!"

"Show me."

Nervously, Perry led the captain back to the kitchen.

"Right here si …" the NCO trailed off. The kitchen table was empty. Empty and overturned. Trooper Daws was lounging on a stool with his feet up on one of its legs. He scrambled up as Small entered.

"At ease," the captain said. "Daws. How long have you been here?"

"I, uh, three minutes, sir? Four?"

"And in that time did you happen to come across a wounded rebel?"

"Um, no, sir. Fairly sure I'd remember that, sir." The trooper grinned, not understanding. Small shot Perry a venomous look.

"Corporal, come with me."

Perry's eyes were fixed firmly on his boots as he was led back out into the hallway.

"What the hell's wrong, Corporal?" Small hissed. His voice was low, dangerous. "Ever since you led us to this house things have gone from bad to worse. First the people living here slip away, then the horses bolt. Now you're seeing goddamn rebs on upended tables. And it's still raining. If you don't—"

A crash interrupted the captain's diatribe. He spun, seeking the source of the noise, but the hallway remained undisturbed.

"What in the name of—" he began, but another crash cut him off. This time it was followed by a third, and a forth. It sounded as though someone was hammering on one of the walls, hammering like a maniac.

Hammering like their life depended on it.

"Who the hell is making all that racket?" Small yelled. He cast around, but could still see no one. And then, as abruptly as it had begun, the noise stopped.

The captain realized he'd been holding his breath. He exhaled slowly, and the look of surprise that so rarely graced his face was swiftly replaced by an altogether more familiar angry glower.

"Hell's teeth, did you hear that Perry?"

"Yes, sir," the corporal answered hastily, as though afraid he was somehow responsible for the disturbance.

"What the hell was it?"

"I ... I don't know, sir."

The captain paced from one wall to the other and back, gimlet gaze surveying the hallway in its entirety. Yet nothing had moved. It had only been the sound, the sound of someone, or something, hammering on one of the walls.

"Did you hear that?" Small called into the living room, where Trooper Fry was laying out his carbine cartridges to dry.

"Hear what, sir?"

"That banging sound?"

"No, sir. You mean the rain?"

"No," Small growled. "How could you not have heard it? It was right here. Were you hitting the walls?"

"No, sir ..." Fry trailed off, looking confused. Small rounded once more on Perry.

"But you heard it?"

"Yes, sir."

The captain glared from one trooper to the next and then, without another word, swept from the room.

Something was wrong here, and Captain Joshua Small was going to get to the bottom of it, one way or another.

Trooper Blake had been assigned to the attic. It was a dust-choked, musty little space of creaking timbers and cloying cobwebs, all dimly illuminated by the light trickling in through the room's porthole window. It was the highest point in the house, overlooking the front yard and accessible only by a rickety stair ladder. Blake had been posted in it to keep watch on the sunken lane approach.

He'd stripped off his dark blue jacket and draped it across the sheet-covered furniture stacked about the attic's corners, hoping that laying it out would help it dry. This done, he planted a chair before the window and sat, staring out into the rain.

Time dragged, and dragged, and dragged. The rain's endless pounding soon began to have a hypnotic effect. Eventually, perhaps inevitably, his eyelids started to droop.

The thunder boomed. No, Blake realized. No. Not thunder. Cannon fire. Twelve pounders, hammering out death and fire and smoke. The rain had stopped. The sun shone and, by its light, the North and the South dealt death over and around Bull Run Creek.

From his vantage Blake watched as a figure stumbled down the lane towards the gate. He was limping heavily, and even at a distance it was clear that his every motion was shot through with pain. As he drew closer, Blake made out the gray and butternut uniform of a Confederate infantryman.

You ought to do something, a tiny voice in Blake's head told him. Get up. Go downstairs. Tell the captain the battle's started. There's a rebel at the gate.

But the rest of his mind shrugged off the voice. He seemed calm, surreally so. Nothing really mattered. All he needed to do was sit and watch.

The rebel opened the gate awkwardly before staggering across the yard towards the front door. The apple tree he passed was whole, the broken branch somehow healed. When had that happened? The rebel was still limping. Indeed Blake now saw that the left leg of his pants was stained dark with blood. Beyond the lane the battle still raged, the distant battalions of gray and blue pounding one another relentlessly. The wounded rebel was fleeing the carnage, Blake realized. Looking for shelter. Little did he realize that the house at the end of the lane was packed with a troop of Union cavalry. He really ought to tell the captain that—

"Someone's coming!"

The man's exclamation came from right beside Blake. He surged to his feet with a startled yell, his numb state shattered as the dream world around him disintegrated.

It was still raining. Blake looked about wildly, embarrassed that he'd fallen asleep on duty. There was nobody beside him. He shook his head, blinked. Outside the yard was deserted, the gate still banging backwards and forwards mournfully. The apple tree's branch was still broken. There was no battle.

But there was something else. Something that hadn't been there before he'd dozed off. Eyes widening, he peered out through the foggy panes.

There were horsemen out there in the rain. Four horsemen, sitting and watching the house—dire, drenched specters in the gray veil. Gray on gray. And, as Blake watched, more gray joined the four. A long, bristling line, emerging from the deluge. Their fixed bayonets glistened.

"Captain!" Blake shouted frantically. "Captain Small! Come quick!"

"What the hell is it now?" Small demanded from below, scrambling up the ladder.

Blake pointed out the window. "Rebels, sir."

"Shit," Small spat as he caught sight of them. "Goddamn shit!"

"Shall I stand the men to, sir?" Cogburn called up.

"What the hell do you think, Sergeant?" Small snapped back. "Tell every man to find a window and check his powder. As soon as those bastards realize they've got us cornered they'll be on us. Hold this window, trooper," he turned to Blake. "Because if the rebels take it and don't kill you, then I will. Is that clear?" Blake nodded. His face was ashen. Without sparing him another glance, Small hastened back downstairs.

Thanks to Trooper Blake's laxness the rebels had them by the throat. Now all they had to do was squeeze.

Throughout the house, Small's troop took to the doors and windows, carbines primed and loaded. The Confederates surrounded them, flooding the fields outside. Ranked up at the very edge of visibility, they formed a dark, silent mass tipped with dripping steel. Their flags hung limp in the rain. They seemed to be waiting, though for what the nervous Union troopers could only imagine.

"There's someone by the apple tree," Perry reported to Small.

"What?"

"Someone ... someone hanging from the apple tree, sir. In the yard."

"Hanging from the apple tree?" Small repeated incredulously. "What in God's name are you talking about now, Perry?"

"Come and have a look, sir," the corporal invited, gesturing to the second story window he was occupying. It looked out over the front yard. Scowling, Small peered out through the grimy panes.

The apple tree stood below him. Its branches were bare and skeletally thin. It looked like some broken old hand, clawing up towards the leaden sky in silent, paralyzed anguish.

And someone was hanging from one of the branches.

Small blinked. No. That branch wasn't even there. It was lying nearby, broken. The tree was quite bare. Nobody there at all.

"You saw it though, sir, didn't you?" Perry whispered. Small turned away from the window, glowering.

"There's nothing out there, Perry. Nothing except the goddamn rebs. Understood?"

Perry only nodded.

Small was halfway back down the stairs when he came face-to-face with a young man. He was tall and gaunt, and wore plain civilian clothes. He paid no heed to Small until the captain physically blocked his route.

"Who in God's name are you?" the cavalry officer demanded. The man looked up, and Small almost recoiled from the sorrow in his eyes. He was young, younger certainly than Small, but in that pale blue gaze there emanated the sadness of a man of greatly advanced years.

"Forgive me, sir," the young man replied in a drained whisper. "I didn't see you." Then, lowering his doleful eyes once more, he slipped past Small. As the captain spun to apprehend him, his outstretched arm brushed only air. There was nobody there.

Small stood on the stairway for some time, silent and still, trying to comprehend what had just happened. When he could not, he continued on his way to the hall, telling himself that he hadn't seen anything. After all, how could he have?

There was nothing there.

It finally happened, just after eight. With a keening yell, the rebels charged.

"Hold your fire!" Small shouted, hastening from one room to the next. "Let them get close!"

That was easier said than done. The Confederate infantry outnumbered the dismounted Union cavalry at least three to one. Like a tide of gray turned black by the sheeting rain they stormed through the muck, crashing over the fence and across the yard.

And yet their advantage was deceiving. Powder soaked, they had no choice but to run at the house with cold steel. And, in the shelter of the hallway, the parlor, the kitchen, the living room and the upstairs bedrooms, the Union carbines were loaded and dry.

"Let them have it!" Small finally bellowed as the rebels closed the last thirty yards. His men opened fire. The house was instantly shrouded in a choking pall of smoke. Men tumbled, throwing up great fountains of mud and rainwater, and those behind slipped and slid as they stumbled over their fallen comrades.

"Load!" Small bellowed. "Load and fire!"

This was what he was here for. This was what they were all here for. They'd trained and drilled, they'd spent the long months in cantonments, they'd ridden the muddy countryside back and forth and now, finally, Captain Small's troop had their first battle. It wasn't how they'd envisioned it. There was no thundering of hooves, no flashing of sabres, no bugle shrilling them to glory or pennants snapping in the wind. Instead there was only mud and rain, and blood, and the stink of gunpowder, and the banshee howls of the enemy as they came at them. But it would do. By God, it would do.

"Keep it up!" Small urged, pacing from one window to the next. There were two men at each, one frantically reloading while the other fired. The discharge of their carbines in the house's confined space threatened to burst the captain's eardrums.

The rebels could not close. Confounded by the mud, blinded by the rain, their own rifles made impotent, they rose like the tide and receded like it, leaving a dozen slumped bodies in their wake.

The Yankees yelled and jeered as they watched the enemy withdraw. They'd done it. Their fingers were raw from slamming home cartridges and yanking back dogheads, their ears rang from one discharge after another, and their throats were sore from the smoke, but they'd done it.

And they soon realized they'd have to do it all again. Back out of range of the Union guns, the rebels were dressing their ranks and reforming.

"Keep your cartridges handy," Small repeated as he passed from one firing group to the next. "Keep a clear eye and keep your cartridges handy." He was shaking, his body thrilling with adrenaline. They'd done it! And they could do it all again!

If the house let them.

Sergeant Cogburn was in the parlor by the front door. Like the captain, he was performing his duties, checking ammunition and trying to grin through his own fear. The men could show it, the NCOs could not.

That was a fact Cogburn found hard sometimes, especially under the command of a captain like Small. His jaw still ached from the officer's blow. He didn't know why the horses had bolted. It wasn't his fault.

But that's not true, was it?

Cogburn knew why the horses had bolted. It was the same thing that was making him want to bolt right now. There was something about this house. It was a purely instinctive sensation. He could feel it coiling in his gut and creeping along his shoulders. He could feel it in the heavy dust that remained, undisturbed, on every surface. He could feel it in the sorrow that weighed on his heart. Why was he sad? So very sad? No matter how hard he tried, he couldn't shake the feeling that he'd lost something, something very dear to him, something that he could never again hold or touch or see or smell.

"Sally, bring water!" The sudden shout made him start. He'd been heading down the corridor towards the kitchen, intending to check on Troopers Daws and Rollens, but the voice made him turn. He barely had time to get out of the way of a pale-eyed young man as he hastened past. He was supporting another man by the shoulder. It took Cogburn a second to realize that the other man wore a gray uniform, and a second more to see that his leg was horribly wounded. He was leaving a trail of fresh blood on the carpet.

Before Cogburn had time to reach out or even speak, the pair were past him and into the kitchen.

"Wait!" Cogburn shouted, dashing after them. Daws and Rollins looked up in surprise as he burst into the kitchen. There was nobody else present.

"Where did they go?" Cogburn demanded.

"Who?" Daws asked.

"The two men. One of them was a reb. They just came in here."

The two troopers glanced at one another, then back to Cogburn.

"We're the only ones here, sir."

Cogburn opened his mouth to reply, but couldn't find the words. He shook his head, turned, and left again.

And tried to tell himself that the trail of old, dry blood staining the corridor's carpet was a figment of his imagination.

"We got movement, Captain!" Trooper Clark called from his post by the front door. Small hurried to his side.

"What is it?" The trooper gestured past the barricade he leaned against.

"Reb officer, sir. Headed this way. He's got a white flag."

Small peered out into the rain, and saw that what Clark said was true. A lone Confederate, mounted, was approaching the house from the lane, a limp white rag held aloft.

"They want to parlay," Small wondered aloud. He felt a fresh surge of excitement. They really must have the bastards cowed if they wanted to discuss terms so soon. "Everyone hold your fire!"

The horseman dismounted at the gate and proceeded across the yard on foot.

"Open the door," Small ordered. "And stay sharp." His troopers had repaired the entrance as best they could, piling a smashed drawing board and a big clothes chest in front of it. Now they pulled them aside for Small to make his way back out onto the front porch.

The rebel was waiting for him.

"Colonel Greaves, 23rd Virginian," the man drawled, offering a hand. "How do you do?"

Small shook the hand stiffly. "Captain Joshua Small, 12th US Cavalry."

Greaves smiled amicably. He was a short man, yet bore the thick beard and mutton chops of a hardened campaigner. His eyes were gray, as gray as his sopping jacket. Behind his lazy smile he looked worn, mournful almost. All of this Small absorbed in an instant. He found himself wondering what the rebel in turn thought of the tall, clean-cut Union officer with the sandy hair and the stony eyes. Greaves' smile gave nothing away.

"Pleased to meet you, Captain Small. How are you boys enjoying this fine part of Old Dominion?"

"My apologies, Colonel Greaves, but I have no time to parlay," Small replied acerbically. The man's sad smile was irritating him, and Captain Small did not like to be irritated. "You initiated this truce. Say what you mean to say."

The colonel's smile remained fixed, apparently unperturbed by Small's brusque tone.

"Well, I just reckoned you boys may quite like to surrender to me and my men sometime soon."

Small scoffed.

"I thought you were the one come here to surrender, Colonel Greaves. Did you not witness your last attack? My men remain unharmed, and you are in no better position than when you started the evening. Withdraw now, while you have the chance."

"No, Captain Small," Greaves said, and though his smile remained unchanged, a chilling note now entered his voice. "You will surrender to me, now. Before it gets dark."

"Why?"

"You don't know where you are, do you?"

"Just north of Bull Run Creek, obviously."

Greaves chuckled, and Small fought to keep his anger in check.

"No, I mean you don't know where you are right now. This house?"

"No. I don't see how ..."

The colonel shook his head, and Small was disconcerted to note the expression in his eyes. Not hostility or enmity, but ... pity.

"There was a battle fought near here not a few months ago, I'm sure you'll recall," Greaves said in an increasingly heavy voice. "What you Yankee boys did to the family that used to live in this here house ... well, it wasn't right. You should leave now, before night comes. I'll accept your surrender with all honors granted."

"Your ruse falls flat, Colonel," Small sneered. "We have the better position, and you know it. We will not abandon this house."

"If you say so, Captain Small," Greaves said. "If you say so. But you'll be out of this house come nightfall, one way or another. Of that you can be sure."

And with that he left, returning to the rain and his men. Small stalked back inside, trying to shake off the colonel's parting message.

One way or another.

Have you seen my daughter?

The words were unspoken, but Blake still heard them clearly. As clearly as though the man was right behind him.

Please, turn around.

What man? Nobody had spoken. There was nobody there. But there was. Blake could feel it. Feel it in the hairs bristling across the back of his neck, in the chill spreading along his spine. Feel it in the hand on his shoulder.

He spun, carbine primed.

"Jesus Christ!" Trooper Rook exclaimed, ducking away from Blake's wild aim. "It's me!"

"How long have you been standing there?" Blake snapped, lowering his weapon.

"I just came up!" Rook protested. "Sergeant Cogburn sent me to check on you. You've been alone up here for hours!"

"I'm fine," Blake said, trying to keep his voice calm and level. "Just fine. Leave me."

He turned back to the window, looking out at the distant shapes of the rain-drenched Confederate infantry, and tried not to think about the young man with the sad blue eyes standing right behind him.

Perry kept hearing the banging noise.

He was posted in the pantry at the back of the house, alone, looking out over the stables. The rebels still hadn't made any move since the first attack, as though they were waiting for something. But Perry had been hearing the banging. It was intermittent and more distant than when he'd first heard it in the hallway. But it was definitely there. Like someone hammering on a wooden door, again and again. It would stop, and Perry would manage to convince himself he'd imagined it just in time for it to start up again.

He'd asked Cogburn if he could hear it when he'd passed by, but the sergeant had said nothing, just hurried on his way. He'd been deathly pale.

And still the banging went on. It started to grate on Perry's nerves. Why could nobody else hear it? Eventually he could take no more. Rising, he abandoned his post and headed for the hallway.

As he drew nearer, the volume of the impacts grew until he could feel the timbers around him shaking. The hallway was deserted. Shouldn't someone be on duty by the window? Perry began to move from one wall to the next, hand brushing the faded paperwork, searching, searching. Finally, he arrived at a point where the tremors of each blow seemed to be greatest, beside the mahogany bookstand. Behind it?

Perry took a breath, and put his shoulder against the stand. With a slow creak it began to shift. And as it did so the source of the impacts began to become apparent.

Perry found himself looking at a door, previously hidden by the bookstand. Someone was on the other side of it, hammering away. Only, as Perry finished shifting the stand, the sound stopped. The door, which had once shaken fit to split, was suddenly still and silent.

Perry swallowed hard and glanced around. Still nobody in sight. He should get back to his post. But something made him stay, made him reach out a brush his hand against the door's handle. Why did he feel so sad? If only he could look beyond the door, maybe that sorrow would be lifted? Slowly, he turned the handle.

There was no one beyond, just dust, and darkness, and the stench of decay. Perry took a breath, and stepped inside.

There was something going on in the yard.

Blake sat up sharply. Had he been dreaming again? No, surely not. There were men outside, men in blue uniforms. From his troop? It didn't look like it. The men were infantry, not cavalry. Were they reinforcements?

They appeared to be escorting someone. A young man. He was struggling with them every step of the way, calling back to the house. Calling up at me, Blake realized. What was he saying? Something … something about his daughter? And a rebel?

The trooper watched as the soldiers halted beside the apple tree. One of the men drew out a rope. Blake realized what was about to happen and, at the same time, realized there was nothing he could do to stop it.

They hanged the prisoner. He dangled and jerked at the end of the rope while the soldiers below jeered and clapped. After several minutes there came a cracking sound, and the branch supporting him snapped. The figure tumbled to the ground, still jerking. One of the Union soldiers stepped in and stabbed down with his bayonet, once. The body twitched. The soldiers laughed and began to disperse, leaving the young man where he lay.

"Dear God," Blake whispered. "So that's what happened to you?"

Even as he watched, reality seemed to collapse. The rain was still hammering down. The dark shapes of the Confederate infantry were still visible in the distance. The Union infantry were gone from the yard, as was the young man's body.

But the broken branch still lay where it had fallen, all those months before.

"Perry?" Small called as he entered the pantry. The rebel answered him with a yell.

The captain barely had time to dodge the man's lunging bayonet. The drenched Confederate scout had crept in through the pantry's broken window. Of Perry there was no sign.

Small snarled and thumped his body into the rebel's, throwing him off balance. The man steadied himself just as the captain drew his sabre. Another stab of the bayonet slid along Small's flank, making him hiss in anger and pain. But now the drenched Confederate had committed to the lunge, and left himself wide open to Small's counter. With an animalistic snarl the captain chopped his blade down into the man's shoulder, severing tendon and hacking into bone.

The rebel screamed and toppled, arterial blood gouting across the pantry floor. Small kicked the shuddering man as he died.

"Bastard," he spat. "Bastard!"

Eventually, the body went limp.

"Perry!" Small roared, storming from the pantry, his sword still red and wet. "Perry, you piece of shit, where are you? Abandoning your post? I'll have you hanged this time!"

He burst into the hallway. It was deserted, but a door he'd never noticed before lay ajar to his right. He made for it, but a voice arrested him.

"I don't think you should go down there, sir."

It was Sergeant Cogburn. He was descending the staircase. Trooper Blake was just behind him.

"What the hell are you doing down here, Cogburn? Get back to your post!"

"Don't open the door, sir," Cogburn said. His voice was heavy, sorrowful, but for once devoid of fear. Small glowered.

"You'll be up on charges when we get back to camp, Sergeant."

"We're not going back to camp, sir," Blake said quietly.

But Small wasn't listening. He'd already opened the door and begun to descend the stairs beyond.

"Captain," Cogburn called, but there was no reply.

It was a cellar, Small realized. A dank, damp little stone cellar, its entrance concealed all along by the bookcase. A tiny slit window, unnoticed at ground level, looked out onto the stable block. Rainwater was gushing in through its cracked panes.

By the watery light Small discovered Corporal Perry down on his knees, hunched over something. He seemed to be in a kind of trance.

"Corporal!" Small snapped. Perry started, turning and rising with the gasp of a swimmer just surfacing from the ocean's crushing embrace.

"Captain," he stammered, looking about with shock. "Captain, I ..."

He trailed off. Small didn't care. He wasn't looking at him anymore. He was looking at the thing the corporal had been crouched over.

It was a corpse. Withered, black scraps of flesh, bound tightly around a framework of yellowing skeletal remains. Ragged tatters of clothing, hanging from the body like the remnants of a shroud. The skull was eyeless, staring up blindly at the low ceiling. Its bony fingers were curled into claws. When the man had died, he'd died in agony.

And his left leg … it was mangled, the bone splintered and crushed.

Left leg, drenched with blood.

"He came here seeking shelter," Cogburn said, right behind Small. The captain spun to find the sergeant and Blake now blocking the route back up into the house.

"He came down the lane during the battle for the creek," Blake elaborated in a sad voice.

"The people who lived here, a young man and his wife and daughter, took him in," Cogburn said. "Only, after the battle, Union troops came here looking for rebels. So the family hid him in this cellar."

"The Union infantry never found him," Blake continued. "But they suspected the owner of the house, the young man. So they took him out into the yard and they hanged him, and when the branch broke they stabbed him to death and drove his wife and daughter out."

"But the rebel was still down here," Perry added, slowly, as though he was only just beginning to understand. "He tried to escape. He hammered and he hammered and he hammered at that door, but there was nobody left to hear him. So he bled to death down here. Alone."

Silence followed the corporal's words. Even the rain had died. Small said nothing for a long time. When he did, his voice was apoplectic.

"That is the most absurd pile of horse shit I've ever heard! All three of you get back upstairs or, by God, I'll shoot you all myself."

"We're not staying here, sir," Cogburn said. Though his voice was quiet he seemed for once quite unconcerned with Small's anger. "We shouldn't be here. It's wrong. He doesn't want us here."

"He's dead," Small almost screamed.

"We're leaving," Cogburn said, beginning to head back upstairs once more. "Come with us, sir."

Small finally snapped. Howling, he lunged at Cogburn. The sergeant half turned in surprise, arm raised instinctively. His elbow caught the captain's chin. There was a crack, and Small reeled backwards, hitting the stone floor hard. He didn't get up.

"Is he dead?" Blake breathed.

"No," said Perry. "Just unconscious."

"Should we take him with us?" Blake asked.

Cogburn shook his head. "He chose to stay here."

"What now then?" said Perry.

"We leave," Cogburn said. "We set the bookcase back in place, we leave and we never come back."

"You want to leave him down there?" Blake said. "He's not dead."

"But how many men are because of him?" Perry responded.

"It's men like him who cause all this misery and suffering," Cogburn said quietly, almost to himself. "Perhaps without him … perhaps without such men the world will know a little more peace."

Colonel Greaves was waiting for them. The rain had stopped, the last golden rays of the dying sun glinting from the tips of the Confederate bayonets.

"Where's Captain Small?" Greaves asked, looking from one face to the next as the troop shuffled out into the yard.

"He elected to stay behind," Cogburn said quietly. Greaves held his gaze for a moment, then nodded. He looked tired.

"Yes. I thought he might."

"You did?"

"Some people just never seem to want to leave the little house at Bull Run Creek. They always stay. One way or another."

DEATH AND TAXES
A. E. Decker

Laughter in a graveyard? Jeck reined Fritter to a halt behind a crumbling stone wall and cocked an ear to the wind. There it came again: whooping. Sounded like Nicky Wilson and Abel Grange, playing some kind of game. Jeck frowned. Didn't they know graveyards were supposed to be *scary*?

Fritter nickered softly and stamped. "You're right, boy," whispered Jeck, reaching down to pat the horse's ink-black shoulder. "We'll teach those boys a lesson. Let's send them screaming back to town."

A shaft of early evening sunlight glinted off the badge pinned to the breast of his ancient armor as he backed Fritter up. *Hello, my name is Jeck and I'm an assassin*, read the curly green letters. He'd made it himself. He gave it a quick polish with his sleeve before digging his heels into Fritter's sides. "Okay, boy. Go!"

Fritter needed no further encouragement. He reared—style mattered—and tossed his mane before breaking into a spirited canter. He surmounted the wall in a single leap and landed with a dramatic thump, gouging deep brown furrows through the soft turf.

Nicky froze in mid-toss, arm extended. Abel missed his catch and the object of their game, a silvery disc, wobbled past him, settling on the newly green earth with a flat-sounding *floomph*.

"Who dares trespass on these hallowed grounds?" bellowed Jeck, aiming his voice so it would reverberate off the mausoleums and shake the fragile jutting tombstones. Sometimes he came to this hill in the middle of the night and practiced yodeling, just so he'd be sure of hitting the right spot. As Fritter reared again, Jeck reached up, plucked his own head off his neck, and hurled it between the two boys.

Graveyard and sky spun in a dizzying kaleidoscope of gray-dotted green and dusty blue as he bounced along the ground, landing face-down in a clump of dandelion. *Oh, poopie. Not quite the effect I'd hoped for.* Sticking out his tongue, Jeck used it to flip himself over in time to see the boys roll their eyes.

"Must you always butt in, Jeck?" asked Abel.

Jeck blinked. "Vwhuht—" His tongue was still sticking out. He slurped it back in and tried again. "What do you mean, butt in? I'm a ghost, this is a graveyard. You're supposed to be scared when you come here, see?"

"No one's scared of you, Jeck," said Nicky, picking at a scab on his elbow.

"Of course you're scared." Jeck dropped his voice to a hollow groan. "Look around, boys. Dead people are—"

"Let's go throw it in MacGrady's abandoned lot." Abel held up the disc.

"Yeah."

They scampered off, footsteps pattering lightly over grass and gravestones.

"—everywhere," Jeck finished to empty space. Quickly rallying, he bellowed after them, "That's right! Flee in terror! BWAH-HA-ha-hahaha … heh."

Silence. Then a thrush started up a happy warbling from the white-flowered perch of a crabapple tree. Doves cooed in the eaves of the Tipton family's granite mausoleum, and a pair of robins spooned in the grass.

"I hate spring," Jeck grumbled. Fritter ambled over and nuzzled his hair. His body, through long years of practice, reached down from the saddle and scooped him back up. He settled himself back on his neck with a properly repugnant snap then sat a moment, tapping a finger against his chin. Eventually, he reached an important decision.

"I need a drink," he declared, and turned Fritter back up the hill towards Albright Castle.

"And then they ran away screaming," Jeck finished. Lifting the bottle, he took another swig of wine. A few drops trickled out around the seam in his neck, but his ether sucked up most of it. Mmm, Riesling.

Maggie's hands continued to knead the massive lump of dough stretched out on the kitchen counter. "Did they?" she asked.

"Oh, yes. Probably wet their pants and everything. I'm sure Abel had a damp patch on his knickers."

"He didn't, did he, Jeck?"

"No." Jeck rolled the bottle between his gloved hands. He never could fool Maggie. "Deep inside they had to be terrified. It'll probably hit them when they're asleep. Probably have nightmares. Don't you think?"

Maggie's lips pursed. She dipped up a handful of flour from the canister and sprinkled it over the dough. "No," she said. She wiped her hands on her apron then leaned against the counter. "No, I reckon they'll sleep pretty well after all that running about."

Jeck hastily lowered the wine bottle he'd just lifted. "But they nearly got killed by a ghost!"

"You threw your head at them. There's hardly anyone in Albright you haven't thrown your head at. Even the biggest fraidy-cat gets used to that kind of thing after a while."

"Used to it?" The world spun worse than it did when he flung his head. "But I'm a headless horseman," he protested. "I have the armor and tattered cape and the spooky deep voice and everything! I ride a big, mean, black ghost horse—"

He followed Maggie's pointed gaze out the kitchen window to where Fritter was indulging in a good roll in the soft grass between the herb beds. All four of his spindly chicken-legs waggled in the air.

Jeck scowled. "Well, he's usually mean. When he's upright." He sucked back wine with a vengeance.

"If you want to start scaring people again, you'll have to make yourself scarce for a while," said Maggie. Taking up a knife, she began cutting the dough into strips.

"Make myself scarce?" Jeck puffed out his chest. His homemade badge gleamed in the kitchen's gaslights. "I'm the official ghost of Albright Castle."

"You gave yourself that title, Jeck. People aren't scared of what they know. And you're ubiquitous."

"Why, thank you."

Sighing, she brushed a lock of damp brown hair out of her eyes. "It means you're everywhere."

"Oh." Jeck deflated a bit. "And that's a bad thing?"

"If you want to scare people it is."

She crisscrossed the strips of dough over the waiting jam tarts then sprinkled them with sugar. Jeck sloshed the last three inches of wine around in the bottle. He knew he should probably listen to Maggie. Being alive herself, she understood the ways of warm, squishy living folk better than he did. *But making myself scarce? Scarce? There's only one Jeck in the world. How much scarcer could I be?*

There had to be another way. He sipped and pondered and by the time he'd sucked the last drop out of the bottle he'd found an answer. "It's my technique that's the problem," he said.

Maggie looked up from checking the oven's temperature. "Your technique?"

"You're right. I've chucked my head at pretty much everyone in town. It's like …" he drummed his fingers against the counter. "It's like the old 'rabbit out of the hat trick.' Everyone's seen it. Now they want to see him pull a crocogator instead."

"Crocodile."

"Crocogator, crocodile, who cares?" he said, waving the bottle dismissively. "You see my point?"

"Yes, but Jeck—"

He jumped to his feet, knocking over his stool. Maggie caught it before it hit the broom propped against the counter and set off a domino-wave of destruction across the kitchen. "All I need is a new act and they'll start screaming again," said Jeck.

"But—"

He handed her his empty bottle. "Thanks, Maggie," he said, patting her coils of brown hair. "You're the bestest."

She huffed. Jeck braced himself to ignore any common-sensical protest. But then she smiled and turned up a hand. "Well, good luck. Come back if you need to chat some more."

Waving his head in cheery farewell, Jeck went to reclaim Fritter from the kitchen gardens.

Peering through the prickly branches of the yew hedge, Jeck watched Rosie, Marion, and Emma skip rope under a dusky blue sky. Their curls bounced as they chanted out numbers, their cheeks pink with exertion. Whoosh, click, whoosh, click; a dreamy rhythm. The piercingly sweet fragrance of a nearby clump of hyacinths added a sharp note to the cool evening air.

Perfect. Smothering a cackle, Jeck pried the lid off the can at his feet and dipped his hand into the brimming red paint it contained. He slapped it across his neck and drizzled it over his shoulders. Some dropped through him and spattered the ground, but enough stained his armor to create a spectacularly gruesome spectacle.

Showtime. Jeck took a deep breath—force of habit, that. "Oo-ohw-woah-ohhhh," he moaned.

"Twenty-one, twenty two ..." On the other side of the hedge, Rosie's skipping faltered to a halt. Emma was probably chewing on her rope handle. Brash Marion just kept going.

"Thirty-six, thirty-seven ..."

Jeck moaned again, louder and more drawn-out than before. Fritter lifted his head from the patch of grass he'd been grazing. Shards of greenery fell through his muzzle. Fritter couldn't actually eat grass anymore, of course, but he kept giving it his best try.

"Oooh-wahoh-woo ..."

"What's that sound?" asked Rosie.

Jeck pushed through the hedge, arms extended, groaning as he went. Unfortunately, he'd forgotten that yew was one of those pesky vegetations that affected ghosts. It bit back.

"Ooo-woao-oh—owie! Owie!" Green needles pierced his ectoplasmic skin. Jeck shuddered. Not with pain precisely—more like his body was being simultaneously stretched and shriveled. Not pain, no; but definitely unpleasant.

Two small hands parted the intertwined branches. A round pink face surrounded by chestnut curls peered in at him.

Jeck stopped struggling. "Um, boo?"

Rosie turned her head to call back over her shoulder. "It's just Jeck."

"Of course it is," grunted Marion, still skipping.

Emma's face joined Rosie's. "Eww, Jeck, what did you do to yourself? You're all goopy."

"It's blood, little girl, blood." Jeck deepened his voice. "The blood of a thousand tortured souls—"

"Is not. It's paint," said Emma with the kind of certainty used to proclaim the end of the world. Too late Jeck remembered her father owned Albright's largest paint-and-wallpaper shop. "Why'd you dribble paint all over yourself, silly?"

"I, um—"

"He was trying to scare us." Marion folded up her rope, exuding boredom.

"Oh." Emma chewed on her rope handle then shrugged. "At least it wasn't the old head-throwing thing again."

An evil gleam came into Marion's eye. Jeck tried to shrink back against the yew as she approached, but the bristles held him fast. "Too bad he didn't," she said. "I'm tired of skipping rope." Her curled fingers reached towards him. Jeck clawed at the branches, but to no avail. She plucked his head right off his neck and held it up. Jeck found himself staring down at Rosie and Emma from a new, high angle. He searched their faces for a trace of fear and found only mild curiosity.

"Let's play catch!" crowed Marion, and Rosie and Emma burst into cheers.

An hour later, the girls' mothers finally called them to come home. "Bye, Jeck," said Marion, dropping his head in the flower bed.

"Bye," he mumbled as she galloped off down the street. At least his body had extricated itself from the yew. After a few mishaps—it stumbled into a poplar twice—it found its way to the flower bed and lifted him from the carnal embrace of a purple hyacinth.

"Poopie," muttered Jeck, reuniting himself. He vowed never to mess with paint again. Some of it had clotted inside him. He shook his leg and a dried spatter dropped onto the ground. After giving the yew a feeling if fruitless kick, he stalked over to Fritter.

"They weren't scared either," he said. Fritter swished his tail as if brushing off a pesky fly and continued tearing up the grass. "Fine. Ignore me." Jeck tapped a finger against his chin. "Well, the bloody corpse idea didn't work, but people are scared of all sorts of things. I'm not finished yet."

He stole a white sheet from Mrs. Dowd's wash line, intending to waft around under it, moaning. That plan definitely would have worked if Mrs. Dowd hadn't caught him sneaking out her back gate. She chased him for seven blocks, yelling, "Give it back, you feather-brained phantom!"

The patrons of a nearby tavern flocked out to the sidewalk to watch. Screaming, yes, but with laughter. They pounded their flagons against the tables, slapped each other on the backs, and had an altogether jolly good time.

Jeck gave up. What was the point if they weren't afraid? "You can have it back," he said, handing the somewhat rumpled sheet back to Mrs. Dowd.

She snatched it then slapped him across the face. His head bounced into the gutter, prompting further hoots from the watchers.

"Smile!" demanded a man in a flower-patterned shirt, quickly scribbling a picture. Had to be a tourist.

"I'm not done yet," muttered Jeck, reclaiming his head.

At midnight, he howled mournfully under Nettie Wishwatch's window. She tossed a basin of water over him and told him to take his noise elsewhere.

Remembering the squeaky study door in George Butler's house, he sneaked inside and eased it open and shut, open and shut. Forty minutes later, George got up in his white nightshirt and cap, fetched an oilcan, tended to the hinges, and returned to bed, all without properly waking up.

He made scary faces in old Mrs. Combly's window. She pulled down the blind.

He flicked the gaslights off and on at the Bullworth's house. "You're disturbing the baby," reproached Mrs. Bullworth.

"Maggie, you've got to help me think of a new trick!"

Her head came off her pillow with a little scream. Her eyes popped open, the whites gleaming in the moonlight filtered through her half-open window.

"Did I just scare you there?" he asked hopefully.

Groaning, she flopped back onto her mattress. "Jeck, it's the middle of the night."

"No, it's four in the morning. You said I could come by if I needed to chat."

"I meant to the castle kitchen, not my bedroom!"

"Nobody's afraid of me, Maggie!" he wailed.

"I know." One hand made little shooing motions. "Take a vacation, Jeck. Why don't you clean up your graveyard? The weeds are eating it alive."

He drew himself up. "I'm a ghost, not a groundskeeper. I like weeds."

"Jeck. Go away."

"But I—"

The pillow she hurled passed harmlessly through him, but Jeck got the message. He stomped to the door. Stopped. Turned. "Just wait," he said in his best spooky sepulcher voice. "By tomorrow I'll have the townsfolk so scared no one will dare go outside after dark ever again."

He tried to slam the door, but it was propped open with a stack of cookbooks and wouldn't budge. He settled for banging his head against the wall a couple times instead. Maggie's soft snores echoed the thumps of his boots down the stairs.

"If I could just scare one person," Jeck said to Fritter as they trotted up the winding, oak-lined path that led towards Albright Castle and the waiting graveyard. The first gray shadows of dawn threatened the sky. "That's all I need to get my momentum going."

Fritter snorted.

"No, really," said Jeck. "One person. Do you see anybody?"

Fritter shook his mane.

"No, I don't either." Jeck sighed.

And then a small noise caught his attention. He tilted his head—carefully, steadying it with a hand. There: a faint creak coupled with a grunt of effort. A *human* grunt. At least one person was awake this early morning.

All right. I asked for one last chance. Jeck shook out his crimson-and-ash cape. He flexed his fingers inside his gloves. "You can do this," he whispered, nudging Fritter in the direction of the sound.

They crept from oak to oak. Away from the path, the grass lay soft and springy underfoot, pebbled with old acorns. A cool, damp breeze hurried past. And there, just ahead, in a little glade, a human silhouette made the final adjustments to a long line that stretched from its neck to the solid branch of a mature oak.

Jeck froze. *Neck, rope, tree, adds up to one big whoopsie!* As the black silhouette climbed onto a box waiting at the foot of the tree, his legs unglued themselves from Fritter's sides. "NO!" he cried, kicking Fritter into a flat-out gallop.

The man's face swung towards him. Eyes the color of raw oysters widened. The foot poised to step off the box trembled in mid-air, exposing four inches of bony ankle sheathed in a holey white sock.

Jeck whipped his sword from its sheath. "DON'T DO IT!" he bellowed. Fritter reared. Branches shook. A rabbit, startled from slumber, bolted for the safety of quieter terrain.

Fritter crashed back to earth. An acorn sprayed out from under one hoof. It struck the man right between the eyes and he nodded, as if this was what he expected from the world.

Jeck re-sheathed his sword. "I mean," he said, in a more conversational tone, "hanging's a dreadful way to go. Even when done properly, you slowly strangle for about three minutes." Crossing his arms over the pommel, he warmed to his tale. "Why, there was this one fellow I remember, took him half an hour to die. Kicking and choking, his bloated tongue hanging out the side of his—"

He broke off then, for the man had turned an even chalkier shade of gray. "Well, you see my point?" he finished.

"Yes, I see." The man nodded, his sharp chin dipping beneath the high collar of his shirt. At last his suspended foot returned to the box's edge. "Someone could find me before I'm dead. Other than you, I mean. Hr-rum ... you're not going to stop me, are you?"

"Stop you?" Jeck laid a comradely hand on the man's shoulder. "I mean to help you."

His long-dead heart sang a hymn of joy. *This* was the chance he needed! Of course people weren't scared of him anymore; he'd gone soft since the old days, back when he was a proper assassin. But one well-decapitated body would put the fear of Jeck into the townsfolk.

"Oh, good." The man sagged in wordless relief. "My apologies for doubting your motives. It's just that most people, when they encounter this, hrm, tableau, feel obliged to talk you out of it."

"I consider that very necrophobic. If a man believes he'd rather be dead, I trust his sense of judgment. After all, it's never done me any harm." Dismounting, he held out his hand. "Jeck the Chipper at your service, sir." Behind him, Fritter lowered his head and began viciously cropping the grass.

The man offered a hand possessing only slightly more flesh than the average skeleton's. Not much warmer either; Jeck rarely needed to blow on his fingers after a handshake. "My name is Rummelmumper," he said. Then added, with the air of getting the worst over, "Obadiah Rummelmumper."

"And that's why you want to kill yourself?" asked Jeck.

"It doesn't help." Mr. Rummelmumper gazed at the sky, his body all joints and angles, like a monochrome crane. "They used to call me Zippy at school," he offered after a moment, with a glum sort of hopefulness.

"That's no reason to hold onto it," said Jeck.

"No." Mr. Rummelmumper sighed. "They didn't, anyway. I just like to imagine there was a time when Zippy would've suited me."

Poor bastard, thought Jeck, who'd used boys like Obadiah as footstools back in his own school days. He felt a sudden urge to pants him, just for old times' sake.

"Why don't you come down off there so we can end your life properly?" he suggested before he gave in to the impulse. "You are ready, aren't you?"

"Oh, yes, certainly." Mr. Rummelmumper clambered down. "How do you want to do this?" he asked, sitting on the edge of the box and beginning to work the noose over his protruding ears.

"Oh, I favor decapitation."

"Decapi—" Mr. Rummelmumper's voice rose to a wince-inducing squeak. He half-stood and the noose slipped back around his neck.

Jeck eased him back down. "Relax. I'm a professional. It'll be over before you feel anything."

"Oh, dear me, yes, you were an assassin in—harrum—your previous … that is—"

Jeck continued patting him in a friendly sort of way. "When I was alive. You'll get used to it soon enough."

"Dear me, so I will. I won't … I mean, do you think I'll rise from the grave?"

Jeck shrugged. "Probably not. You're barely alive now, after all. Is that a problem?"

"Oh, no." Mr. Rummelmumper shuddered. "I'd just as soon stay dead. Graveyards are so wonderfully peaceful, you know."

Hidden in the branches of an oak, a lark trilled. Jeck's attention shifted to the sky, which was taking on the appearance of ink that someone had poured a large amount of water into. "We'd better get on with your decapitation. I go kind of insubstantial-ly during the day. Unless you'd rather put it off until tonight?"

"Gracious, no." Mr. Rummelmumper squeezed his eyes shut. "They'll be bringing them to my house today, you know."

"Them?"

"In boxes. Thousands of the ghastly things. They'll drop them in my parlor. Thud, thud. Like nails being driven into a coffin. Oh, my." He opened his eyes. "Coffin. I quite forgot to order one."

"Someone might have gotten a bit suspicious if you had." Jeck took another glance at the sky, already perceptively lighter towards the east. "I'm sure your family or friends or some sympathetic agency will pick out a nice one for you. Now shall we get on with it?"

"Of course. So sorry." Mr. Rummelmumper knelt, laying his head on the box's edge. "Would this be convenient for you?"

"Just fine." Jeck bounced on his heels to limber up. "I used to do most of my work from Fritter's back, you know. Much trickier." Fritter lifted his head at the sound of his name. His sleek black hide had paled to a slatey gray under the encroaching dawn. "Good old days, eh, boy?" Jeck called to him then focused on Mr. Rummelmumper. "Any last words?"

Mr. Rummelmumper gave this due consideration. "What were yours, Mr. Jeck?"

"'Choose the steak, guys.' And then I think I belched, but that doesn't really count."

"Pardon?"

"Advice for my fellow prisoners. The last-meal chef was not all he was cracked up to be. I don't think it's relevant here."

"No." Mr. Rummelmumper repositioned his head on the box. "How about 'sorry for being a bore?'"

"That'll do," said Jeck. He drew his sword.

And only then did he remember.

Heat welled up from the soles of his boots, suffused his body, and boiled into his head until by all rights steam should have poured out of his ears. He didn't need to look down to know he'd literally turned red.

He cleared his throat. "This is very embarrassing," he said.

"What?" asked Mr. Rummelmumper. "You haven't forgotten how to do it, have you?"

"Of course not. It's just that ..." He cleared his throat again and wished he hadn't. It sounded feeble, apologetic. And really, it wasn't his fault. "The captain of the guard," he said.

He'd meant it as an explanation, but Mr. Rummelmumper shot upright. "Where? Has he spotted us?"

"No, he's not here. I mean," Jeck just managed to stop himself from clearing his throat a third time. "He confiscated my sword."

Stupid captain. Big, pale-haired bastard, saying some folderol about how he'd, well, lose his head and take a swipe at someone if he were allowed to keep it. What nonsense.

The lark trilled again, with more confidence this time. Slowly Mr. Rummelmumper sat up. "You don't have a sword."

"I have a wooden sword," Jeck corrected. He flourished it and the flimsy blade wobbled in its hilt. Steadying it with a hand, he sent a hopeful smile at Mr. Rummelmumper. "We could give it a try."

"Give it a try? That glorified toothpick couldn't cut soup!"

"Hey, now, there's no need to be rude," said Jeck, patting the sword just in case its feelings were hurt. Some of the silver paint flaked off.

Mr. Rummelmumper picked up the discarded noose and began

working it over his ears again.

"What are you doing?" Jeck grabbed the rope.

"Serves me right for trusting a headless ghost." Mr. Rummelmumper tried to shove him away and adjust the noose at the same time. "I'm going to finish this before the captain does show up."

"It's not my fault if I mix things up occasionally," said Jeck, getting a grip on the noose. "*You* try thinking clearly when your brain's been severed from your spinal cord."

"Death by hanging's sounding better by the moment!" Mr. Rummelmumper lashed out with a foot, but Jeck dodged it.

"Look, if you could just wait a minute, I'm sure I could find a pocket knife—"

"You're proposing to cut off my head with a pocket knife?" Mr. Rummelmumper managed to pull the noose under his left ear. The rest got stuck under his nose.

Jeck clung to the rope like a stinkbug. "All right, an ax. There are plenty of woodcutters outside the city."

"That'll take ages!" Tears rolled down Mr. Rummelmumper's cheeks and dripped off the knotted fist of his chin. "I must do it this morning."

"But if you hang yourself, it won't enhance my reputation as a terrible scary ghost!"

The first rays of sunlight brightened the oaks' leaves to a soft green. Another lark joined in the morning song. Also, oddly, a duck that had just wandered into the grove. Fritter took one look at it and bolted to the far edge of the clearing, white-eyed and snorting.

A duck. Jeck's hand clenched around the rope until the tortured fibers shrieked. Then he erupted. "You are *not* afraid of ducks, Fritter! You can't be! You're a big, mean black horse!" He hurled his sword across the clearing and the duck scrambled into the air. Fritter shied again and Jeck glared. "What's the matter with the world?" He swung back 'round to Mr. Rummelmumper, who'd been feebly trying to pry his fingers off the rope all this while. "Do I scare you?" he demanded.

Mr. Rummelmumper burst into tears. The rope pulled free of Jeck's slackened grip, but he continued sobbing into his cupped hands, his bony shoulders shaking with the force of his grief.

"There, there," said Jeck. He patted Mr. Rummelmumper's knobby back, but the man kept crying. Overhead, the sky took on distinctly blue tints. "What did I say wrong?" asked Jeck as a chastened Fritter came over and nuzzled his hair. "I only wanted to know if I scared you. Ghosts should be scary."

"Then I wish I were a ghost." Mr. Rummlemumper gulped and rummaged through a pocket. He came up with a starched white handkerchief and mopped his face. "Everyone's afraid of me."

Jeck froze.

Mr. Rummelmumper had a good blow, checked the contents, then tucked the kerchief back in his pocket. "Especially in spring, when those dreadful *things* arrive." A shudder shook him from head to heel. "Why, last year, one man fainted away on his doorstep after he saw who'd rung the bell."

"Just at the sight of you?" Seizing Mr. Rummelmumper's lapels, Jeck shook him until his teeth rattled. "Without moans, sheets, or a flaring red cape? Without being headless, or for that matter, dead? What's your secret?"

Mr. Rummelmumper blinked. The birds sang in full chorus now, and the sun's rays had brightened from a weak lemon yellow to burnished gold. Jeck's strength was fading fast. He shook Mr. Rummelmumper again. "Speak quickly, man."

Mr. Rummelmumper's lips moved. Jeck bent over him, holding onto his head so it wouldn't fall off. Fritter's ears pricked, as if he wished to hear the secret as well.

The explanation didn't take long. And when Mr. Rummelmumper finished, Jeck smiled.

"I hope Jeck isn't here," said Nicky as he and Abel trudged up the graveyard hill.

"He's such a pain," Abel agreed, spinning the flying disc around one finger.

Both turned their heads at a rustling sound, expecting to see Jeck emerge from between two tombstones, perhaps wearing a sheet or covered in red goo. But the interloper was a thin man in a tight black suit pushing a wheelbarrow. He hummed a jaunty tune as he knelt and began clearing the weeds from Mrs. Toomey's tombstone.

Both boys stared. "Who are you?" asked Nicky.

The man chuckled and arranged a bouquet of fresh hyacinths on the grave. "Call me Obie. I'm the new groundskeeper here."

Abel squinted at him, the flying disc hanging forgotten off his finger. "Say, I know you, mister. Aren't you the—"

"Groundskeeper," said Obie firmly. His knees crackled as he stood and held out a hand. "Mind if I give that thing a toss?"

* * *

Mr. Grange had just settled into his chair when the doorbell rang. "Martha?" he called, but she was out back hanging up laundry. Sighing in annoyance, he laid down his pipe and went to the door.

An armored figure stood on the stoop, a sheaf of papers tucked under one arm. It lifted its head—was that a seam around its neck?—and a creepy grin spread over its face.

"Good evening, Mr. Grange. I'm here to speak to you about the money you owe for the past year."

Mr. Grange paled and clutched the doorframe for support.

Jeck smiled. The fresh breeze came again, setting his cape to billowing and snapping. Ah, the rich taste of fear. What a splendid season, spring.

A shaft of early evening sunlight glinted off a little badge pinned to his chest. *Hello, my name is Jeck and I'm a taxman*, read the jagged red letters.

☠

"WHAT IF IT COULD SPEAK!"
Terence Kuch

"Par vivo—Par che senta—E che voglia parlar!"
—Don Giovanni, Act II

————————◆————————

Another hammer blow quakes the stone. Marble chips scatter on the workshop floor, white against bare dark wood. The stone-hewer is unhappy. He curses—in poor Italian because he is from the provinces, not from here. He has broken the pommel off my sword.

"Now how do I fix this?" he mutters, prowling chaotic shelves.

"Nino!" he calls out. A boy appears, chewing remains of food. The sculptor beckons to him. "Come here!" he says. "Look there!" He sweeps an arm toward the shelves. "Where in God's name is ..." A pause. "Aha!" he says. "Never mind." He lifts a pot and brings it toward me, studies how to apply its glue to my sword. He smears it on, wipes off the excess.

"He won't care," he says to himself, nodding at me. "The dead ones don't need swords, anyway." He smiles. "Especially not the great Commendatore! Eh, Nino? How does he look?"

The apprentice tells him that the repair looks just fine; the town magistrates will never notice. They know nothing of art, he says, only money.

The statue-maker nods, stands back, admires his work, selects a chisel, tests its edge, picks up his favorite mallet. He goes to work again, more carefully now, smoking, swearing, blaming the stone, blaming the town for buying such cheap stuff for him to work with, full of cracks and flaws, not worthy of such a one as him, *il grande*, the renowned sculptor Massimo. The better grade of dead man, he says, gets better stone like that miserable artist Bernini gets for the ones he carves, that he insists on, that makes that wretched turdson so famous.

"That's the secret: good stone," he mutters. "It's easy after that. And tools. Good tools. Pay me more, I get better tools!"

Nino sits dutifully near the door, waiting for his master's next command. Occasionally he makes rude gestures behind the older man's back.

Gradually, with each chisel-stroke, each riffler-tap, I remember more of who this stone was, who I was in life. Memories are coming back to me, a few days or weeks at a time.

The statue-maker swears at me each time he cuts not quite where he meant to, which is often. He picks up a rondel, turns it around gimlet-eyed, sighs, puts it down, picks up another.

"Commendatore!" he says to me, "these miserable stinking town officials pay me only five *piastre* to carve you, those chiselers!" He realizes the unintended pun, laughs bitterly, spits on what he says, by next Friday, will be my face. "That fool of a faker Bernini gets ten gold *ducati* just for a head!"

Angrily, he gouges into the stone where neck will be, nose, mouth. Gradually, my face and head take shape; clothes and boots; hands; sword, its pommel-break disguised from inexpert view.

I see. I hear. Perhaps, some day, I will be able to speak.

I see my emerging form reflected in Massimo's eyes; it is something like him, but larger, more noble. And I see other shapes around the workshop, stone in various stages of being-carved, or sadly, being-abandoned. Some look human, but there are also dolphins, eagles, dragons, imagined shapes of Jesus, Zeus, or Galatea: impossible forms of god and man.

Are these aware, like me, of who they were or who they will become?

I am stone.

There was a flesh-and-blood Commendatore, it seems, who looked like the clay maquette Massimo has made, that he carefully studies before mapping a measurement onto me. A soldier, I think; otherwise, why the sword? And from conversations in the workshop I gather that the town council has agreed to pay—but not too much—a sculptor—whose work is not too dear—to commemorate him—but not too well—in stone.

So I am to look as the Commendatore did in life. Is he coming back to life through me? I have memories of one I might have been. Indeed, they grow clearer each day; but they seem as told to me, not lived. I am not yet the Commendatore. Perhaps I will be, if I am not set aside, like others here, to dust and stillness.

Massimo spots a few stone-bruises he has made through haste and ineptitude, through holding a chisel at the wrong angle. He swears in the name of God and several saints, polishes them off laboriously. Then, at last, the statue is finished. Massimo stands back, frowns, nods, shrugs, puts his tools down, brushes the last stone-dust from my form, takes off his leather apron, mutters, "Better than five *piastre* deserve, old man!"

He opens the workshop door, calls impatiently. Four burly men enter, banging the door behind them. They try to lift me off the workbench, but I am heavy. The cart-man is summoned, comes. He and Massimo and the burly men lift, carry, load me onto the back of a wagon, the sculptor complaining the while of the men's carelessness with his priceless object. They ignore him.

The horse is whipped, strains. The wagon moves. I am staring straight up into the bright Italian sky. Three clouds pass, one after another, and five tree-limbs. Then the churchyard.

The men pull me off the wagon, carry me through a gate set in a wall, place me none too gently on a freshly set, low pedestal. There is a bronze plaque on the pedestal, but from my position I cannot read it. Two dates, no doubt birth and death, and "loving husband of," or "loving father of." But my memories tell me an only child, my daughter, died after being seduced by some minor noble. Of shame, her hand on the hilt of a dagger.

The men stand back, hands on hips, tilt their heads, mutter, "ah ..." "aha ..." "ah ..." until one says "It's straight enough." Massimo tells them it isn't straight enough. There is arm-waving and reddened faces, but 'straight enough' seems to win. Then they all leave.

Alone now. The wind calms, is still. Tree-leaves hang motionless. I feel, very gradually, the earth under me move so gently that only one as still as I could feel it on its way to where land gives way to ocean, and ocean, land. And in the quiet I feel the presence of small, mindful things crawling in the earth. They want to eat, to mate, to avoid the jaws of something larger.

The next day, Massimo enters the churchyard, stands in front of me, frowns, shifts foot to foot, notes the position of the sun several times, listens for the church-rung hours. Finally, two men dressed in long dark robes and trinkets of office appear. He calls them "magister." They ignore him, walk around me head tilted, a-ha-ing and a-hum-ing just like the cart-man did but with more-refined pronunciation, whispering together. Finally, one pulls a money-bag from his belt, counts out four *piastre* into the sculptor's impatient hand. A very loud argument ensues, with Massimo stamping up and down and the magistrates pointing to me several times and shaking their heads. One takes a standing-up-straight posture and then leans to one side. Finally, Massimo takes the money and stalks away, making the *figa* gesture and advertising loudly the moral flaws of their mothers. Once he is out of sight the officials laugh and slap their knees.

I am alone again. There is a different kind of silence, now: wind, water-drops falling lightly on me. I remember it as rain, how it had felt on the Commendatore's skin. But this sensation is different for me; it is not the same rain.

Again it is day. Then it is night. Then it is day again; how many, I do not know.

In the graveyard, glue weakens. The pommel falls off my sword, leaving a rough, stained spot where the glue, poor cheap stuff, has lost its hold.

After a time, I attend to the statues near me. They are as still as I. At first, there is no way of knowing if they wonder, as I do, who they are, what they are doing here. But gradually I come to feel their minds, the minds of these statues. Each feels something else also, that I do not. What is it?

After many days, perhaps, I feel it, too: under each pedestal, a corpse. Under mine, the dead soldier; one who is me, but not me; what remains when the ghost, the soul, the spirit has gone to its place of judgment. But if the Commendatore is here, beneath me, then who am I? I, who thought I was the Commendatore himself come to wan life as stone. So I am not he, after all, but mere simulacrum; the stone image of a life.

But now, suddenly, my moldering thoughts are interrupted by shouts, whispers in the dark from beyond the churchyard wall. Confused shouts of "This way!" "No! That way!" Thudding of feet. Then, from the other side of the wall, heavy breathing, a muffled laugh. Shouting fades.

A laughing man leaps the wall, passes near me, rests his back against a tree. He stops laughing. He is impatient. He twists his fingers. His eyes flick around. Minutes pass. Then a second man laboriously surmounts the wall, joins the first. They speak, with skill and rough approbation, of women they ruse and use, and mention, by name or rank, the men who fail to guard them.

Something is moving beneath me: a force. It stirs. I seem to know this man, but not I; the Commendatore knows him, with hatred. About his daughter, a rape, a fight, an unexpected blow. About death.

We recognize Don Juan, the man who killed me, and his fool.

The ghost of the Commendatore, his spirit, erupts upward from the corpse. Inside me, it moves; it whips my tongue into speech. We make a sound, a cry of rage. I utter a woeful line: "Woe, woe to the Don this night!" I did not know until then that I could speak. What else is within my power now? Or is the power mine?

The Don looks around. "Who said that?" he says, drawing his sword.

"A spirit!" says the second man, trembling.

The Don ignores him, says again, "Who said that?" He waves his sword toward the statues.

"Leave the dead in peace!" the Commendatore says through me, and now the Don sees it is my form that speaks. In spite of Massimo's indifferent work, he recognizes, in the lines of stone, my face.

"Aha," he says, "the Commendatore!" He sees the bronze plaque on my pedestal, turns to the second man. "Read it, my good fool! Tell me what it says."

"Ah, Master," says the fool, backing away, "it's too dark to read that thing by moonlight."

I wonder why the Don doesn't just read it himself. There is a brief dispute. Then the fool inches sideways toward me, ready to bolt. He kneels, looks at the plaque, squints. His lips begin to move. I, too, am curious as to what the plaque says. The fool looks up in terror, backs away, whispers, "It says—'On the one who slew me—Vendetta!'"

He is trembling again, not very healthy for a man his age. The Don, however, puts his head back, laughs, looks me straight in the eye. "Oh, very funny!" he says, sarcastically.

Inside my breast, the Commendatore's rage knows no bounds.

Hands on hips, the Don studies my form, moves to turn away. But then, a strange light in his eye, he says to the fool, "Invite him for supper tonight! Invite the statue!"

"Are you mad?" the fool shouts. "My God, can't you see the terrible look it's giving us? *Par vivo—Par che senta!* It's alive! It hears us!"

The Don insists, and after much wheedling and threat the fool approaches me, bows deeply, sighs, kneels.

"O noble statue," he begins,

"O great commander

"Marble-wrought,

"My master (not I!—not I!)

"My master

"Bids thee

"Sup with him this night."

I think I am not much interested in such an invitation, but we nod our head, the Commendatore and I.

"O Lord!" says the fool, "he nods his head!"

The Don, now assured from rebuff, approaches me himself. "Tell me now with your own lips: Will you sup with me this night?"

Suddenly I speak. We answer, "*Yes!*"

The Don turns theatrically, twirling his cape. He shouts "Prepare the feast!" and the two leave.

We are alone. "*Yes!*" the Commendatore says again, with satisfaction.

Now I know what I was meant for: to give the Commendatore a last strength, the strength of stone. He will go to the banquet. He will have his revenge. I feel the ghost taking control, thrusting me aside as a crude artifact no longer needed. The Commendatore appreciates the statue's commanding weight, flexes its ponderous legs.

"Now to be stone," he says grimly, "Now to be stone."

PUSHED OUT
Jay Wilburn

———— • ◆ • ————

Being dead is not going to keep me from watching out for my wife and children, he thought.

He was surprised he could still think. Dying was confusing and it took a while for him to wrap his mind around it. He found himself back in the kitchen. He had not died there and he did not remember his death the way he remembered playing catch with Hank who had just turned four. He couldn't pull up the final event of his life in his mind the way he could remember Tommy getting sick on ice cream at the Pirate Putt Putt Arcade on his tenth birthday the previous summer. He had no feeling attached to his actual death the way he got scared teaching Kim to drive before she got her license on her sixteenth birthday.

He felt sad and confused standing in the middle of his kitchen not feeling the rug under his feet or the air coming from the fan spinning above his head. He tried to look up at the spinning blades. It was on high. He could hear papers being rustled on the counter.

You're wasting power, he thought. *That's too high.*

He liked to watch the fan until it seemed like the blades were moving backward. It was an illusion he enjoyed since he was a kid. But even on high, he was seeing each blade moving around in a smooth motion. There was no optical illusion for him to draw comfort or nostalgia from.

I guess you need eyeballs for optical illusions, he thought, *and a life.*

He had trouble keeping connected to the floor while staring at the fan. He saw the fan slow down just before he looked away and leveled himself in the middle of the kitchen. The papers stopped rattling.

He looked around and saw his wife standing at the toggle switch.

See, baby, I told you that was worth installing.

She was looking at him as she crossed the kitchen. She stumbled on the edge of the rug. He reached out to catch her, but he had no arms. She walked on within inches of him. He tried to smell her, but there was no sense there either.

He turned and saw Doris sit down at the counter. It was piled with food he had not seen before that point. There was another woman sitting across from Doris. Doris's hair looked more gray and frazzled. The other girl was blond and young.

As he looked at his wife's hair, he thought, *You look so old, Doris. How long have I been gone?*

The girl said, "They bring so much food don't they?"

She is from the church. I remember her from the church. She works with Tommy... and Kim when she goes. I don't remember her name.

Doris said, "Yeah, people don't know what to do so they cook. Do you want some of this? I don't have room for it all. The kids hardly eat casseroles ... except Hank. He eats anything."

"I'll eat some with you. You should eat," the girl said.

That's good. Get her to eat and lay down maybe.

"I couldn't," Doris said.

She was staring at the cabinets next to the stove.

"Do you want to lay down, Doris," the girl asked. "I can put this stuff away and look out for the kids while you sleep."

Never go away, blond girl from church.

Doris kept staring at the cabinets. "Al used to take care of that."

My name is Al, he thought. He felt afraid, but wasn't sure why.

"The food?"

Doris looked back at the girl and then under the counter. "No, the lights. I don't even know how to change those bulbs."

Oh, hell, I meant to do that before ... well, I meant to do lots of things before.

The girl dug through the drawers.

The bottom drawer.

She kept looking in the top drawers.

"Do you know where they are?"

"Al handled it."

They are in the bottom damn drawer!

"They are in the bottom drawer, Mommy."

Doris looked down under her stool behind the counter. She lifted little Hank up into her lap and wrapped her arms around him. She rested her lips on top of his sweat-matted head as he rubbed at his eyes.

The girl said, "Great job, Hank, they're right here."

She began unscrewing the case and slid out the tiny bulb from the socket. "How did you get to be such a smart little boy?"

"My daddy," Hank folded his arms on the counter and laid his head on them away from his mother's mouth.

The women looked at each other for a moment and then looked at other things in the kitchen.

"There we go."

As the light flicked on, she screwed the cover back into place.

"You need a place to live, Kate?"

Kate is her name. Damn it, I knew that.

"Not just yet, but I'll keep checking on you and the kids, I promise."

"That's sweet of you."

"Mommy," Hank said pointing up from the counter, "the fan is going backwards. Look. Oh, it stopped. Watch it."

"The fan doesn't go backwards, Hank," Doris said.

It does when you have eyeballs, Al thought.

Hank laughed. "Where's Daddy?"

Kate started putting away dishes over beside the refrigerator. Doris looked up at the fan and blinked.

I'm right here, buddy. Always right here.

"Daddy's still in Heaven, son, and he'll be there waiting for us when we go a long, long time from now."

Hank said, "No, Mommy, I heard him. You and Katie and Daddy were talking in the kitchen and it woke me up. Where is he?"

Holy shit, Al walked toward the counter and looked closely at Hank's face. He was looking past Al. *Can you hear me, buddy?*

"You were dreaming, honey."

"No, Daddy was using bad words and he was mad about the light bulbs."

Hank, can you hear me? Hold up four fingers for four years, if you can hear me.

"Hank it was a dream … just a dream. Do you hear me?"

"Yes, I hear you," he said.

One of the dishes dropped and broke. Kate screamed. Al turned around and saw the kitchen was dark and the refrigerator was closed. Kate was gone. He turned back and saw the counter was empty. Hank and Doris were gone. He looked up and saw the fan was off. The only light was from the tiny lights under the counter shining on the dirty dishes in the sink and the clean stovetop. The new light was shining brighter than the others.

Remember, the bottom drawer, Hank. Remind your mother.

Al heard Hank cry from upstairs. He walked around the counter and stopped at the foot of the stairs. He looked down at nothing and then up the stairs.

What if I walk right through and fall into hell?

He heard Hank cry again. Al took a step and rose up with it even though he could not feel it. He continued up one step at a time. He heard one of them pop. He imagined stepping on it again, but nothing happened. He felt for the rail, but didn't sense it. He continued up until he reached the top. Al turned around and looked back down. He felt off balance and backed away from the stairs.

Al reached the boys' room. He looked back at the master bedroom. He started to peek through the door at the darkness inside.

"What's going on out there?" Doris yelled.

Al backed away.

Tommy yelled back, "Hank's having bad dreams. Everything is fine."

Al tried to push on the boys' closed door and found himself inside. Hank's clown nightlight and Tommy's phone were the only light.

You need to sleep for school tomorrow, Tommy. Are you going back to school yet?

Tommy sighed.

Al asked, *Can you hear me, Tommy?*

Tommy kept playing the game on his phone and ignored his dad. Al couldn't decide if that was any different than usual. Hank stirred again under his twisted sheets. Al walked over and knelt beside Hank's bed. He smelled urine. He reached down and felt the sheets were wet under him. The smell and sensation of touch were gone before Al registered that any sensation at all was unusual now. It was like watching the fan spin backward. Once he realized it was happening, the illusion was gone.

Hank has wet his bed. Go get your mother, Tommy. Tommy, go get your mother.

The crash and beep from his game continued quietly.

Hank whimpered. "Don't tell."

Al looked back at Tommy leaning against his wall on his bed with his knees up. The boy glanced up from the light off his screen and then back down.

I know you can smell that, Al demanded. *Hell, I can smell it and I don't have a nose. Once I figure out how to grab things, that phone is vanishing.*

Hank whimpered and twisted in his wet sheets again. "No, Daddy, don't, please."

Tommy said, "Go back to sleep, Hank. It will be better in the morning."

Probably not, Al said.

Hank started crying again.

I'll be here with you, Hank. I will always be here.

He tried to make his imaginary hand reach out to hold his son's shoulder. Hank shivered in his wet sheets.

Al found himself standing in the kitchen again. The fan was rustling the papers on the counter. He felt nothing and he missed it. He didn't look up because it made him feel loose from the earth and he was having trouble holding on even without staring at the whirling blades.

"You need to tell me when that happens," Doris said as she poked at the buttons on the microwave.

Al turned toward the beeping noise.

Hank answered from under the curved end of the counter. "Yes, Mommy."

Al turned back and saw his son looking out of the shadows sucking on three of his fingers.

He hasn't done that in over a year ... wetting the bed or sucking his fingers.

Doris opened the microwave door and slammed it back again. The beeping continued.

"You shouldn't just lie in it all night. I'm right across the hall. Tommy can come with you to get me."

Hank took his fingers out of his mouth. "Yes, Mommy."

He tried to call you. You and Tommy weren't listening.

"Don't fight," Hank said.

Doris finally hit the start button and the microwave began to hum and spin the carousel plate under the light. "I'm not mad at you, honey. You're just too big of a boy to start wetting your bed now."

He just lost his father. Give him a break, Doris.

"Don't tell anyone," Hank slid down with his back against the cabinet underneath the counter.

"Well, don't start doing this again, honey."

What are you saying, Doris? Come on. You have to understand how he must feel.

Doris placed the tea pitcher under the faucet and worked the arm up and over for cold. The arm snapped off and water sprayed into the air hitting the fan blades. Doris and Hank screamed.

Hank yelled. "No, Daddy, don't do it."

I didn't do this, Al said.

"Hank, go get Tommy. Hurry!" Doris shouted covering her face.

Hank ran into the living room screaming with his hands over his head like a cartoon character of himself. Al actually laughed. Water began to wash through his vision. It was disorienting, so he backed away from the spray.

The valve is under the sink. Shut it off, Doris.

Tommy ran through Al and the water into the kitchen. His feet slid out from under him and he slammed into the edge of the sink, knocking his mother into the front of the refrigerator. The water caught Tommy full in the face. Doris handed him a metal bowl and he forced it down over the water. The spray blasted loudly off the inside of the bowl. The stream washed across the counters and behind the stove. It soaked into the fabric of the toaster cozy Al had inherited from his mother.

I wonder if she is around somewhere. Could I even see her? It would be nice to have someone to talk to ... that can talk back, Al thought. *The shutoff valve is under the sink. Come on, Tommy. I told you this.*

Doris ran across the kitchen and reached for the phone. She slipped and fell on her back under Al at the edge of the counter. He reached down for her, but felt nothing as he looked into her twisted face and wet, gray hair. She groaned and closed her eyes.

"Mom, are you okay? Mom? How do we turn it off?"

The valve under the sink, damn it!

"Stop fighting," Hank called from the living room.

"Shut up," Tommy yelled back over the roar of the water in the bowl.

Hank, come here, Al yelled.

"No, it's all wet," Hank answered.

"Mom?" Tommy called.

As Doris lay in the floor moaning, Al left the kitchen and maneuvered into the living room. He still went around the furniture.

He arrived and found Tommy sitting on the couch next to Hank. Tommy was playing videogames. Hank was hugging his knees and watching. Al stared at Tommy for several seconds before he spoke to Hank.

Hank, it's Daddy. I need you to go in the kitchen ...

Al looked at Tommy again and stopped talking.

"I'm not supposed to go in the kitchen," Hank said without looking away from the T.V.

"I know that, dummy," Tommy said thumbing the controller.

Al tried to look at the TV, but the screen looked scrambled and disjointed. He felt like he was tilting until he looked away.

I guess I need eyeballs for this too, Al said. *Don't call him a dummy.*

"No," Hank cried covering his ears and closing his eyes. "Don't take his eyes, please."

Tommy said, "Shut up, Hank. This isn't that kind of game."

Al said, *Listen to me, Hank. This is important. Go tell Mommy that the shut off valve is under the sink.*

"I don't understand," Hank whispered with his eyes still closed and his hands over his ears.

"Just watch and learn the game then," Tommy said.

Hank, go to the kitchen and tell Mommy to look under the sink. Go right now.

Hank moaned and stepped off the couch.

Tommy called after him without looking away from the television. "You're too young to play. Don't go telling on me, dummy."

Don't talk to him like that, Al yelled.

Hank ran to the kitchen covering his ears and screaming. Al followed after him.

"Stop screaming, Hank," Doris said.

Hank moaned some more. Al followed behind him and put his hand on Hank's shoulder. He could feel the fabric and warmth for a second and then it was gone.

"Look under the sink," Hank yelled covering his ears.

Doris said, "Go back in the living room like I told you or you're in big trouble, little man."

Al walked around the counter. Hank sat in the floor.

Honey, the valve is under ... what the hell?

Al looked under the sink and saw legs sticking out from the open doors.

Doris said, "Hank, are you wetting the floor? I just mopped in here."

Hank cried, "Don't tell anyone. You have to look under the sink or he'll take our eyeballs."

Doris reached down and snatched Hank up as she walked him out of the kitchen. "I'll be right back, Mark, sorry."

"I'm fine," the man under the sink said. "I'll be done here soon."

Al looked up at the faucet arm. The entire apparatus was new. He looked over and saw his mother's toaster cover was missing. He knelt down and tried to look under the sink.

That seems like a lot of work to fix a broken faucet, Mark.

Al smelled urine again and felt the air from the fan. He turned and looked at the puddle in the floor where Hank had been.

"Mark, do you want more bread?" Doris asked from the other side of the counter.

A man answered, "No, thank you, I'm good."

Al looked back at the closed doors under the cabinet in the dark. He looked up at the unmoving fan. He looked down at the floor and saw the puddle had been cleaned.

Al walked out of the dark kitchen into the living room. A man was sitting in Al's spot next to Doris. His seat was occupied by the broad shouldered man with dark hair and a tanned bald spot.

At least he's bald, Al said.

Hank laughed and choked on his juice. Kim pushed her spaghetti around her plate as she texted on the phone in her lap. Tommy was rolling pasta on his fork.

"Calm down, honey, Eat slowly." Doris said.

Her hair was neatly up for the first time since Al found himself in the kitchen without a body. The gray was gone.

You're dyeing now, Doris? Al asked.

"No," Hank yelled dropping his fork in his spaghetti.

"Don't talk back to me, Hank."

"Don't hurt my mommy," Hank yelled.

"Hank," Doris yelled, "Go to your room and sit on your bed until I tell you to come back."

Hank slid out of his chair and walked to the stairs with his head down.

"I'm sorry about that, Mark, he's had a tough time since ... everything," Doris said.

You won't even say my name?

"That's fine," Mark said. "He's a good kid. All of them are."

Tommy and Kim didn't look up.

Al walked slowly to the stairs. As he mounted them with his unsure, disembodied balance, Tommy spoke behind him.

"Hank pissed the chair again, mom."

"Tommy, we have company."

"That's okay, Doris, I'll get it."

Al wavered as he tried to look back, so he just faced forward as he moved after Hank.

"No, Mark, I'll get it. Thank you. I'm sorry about all this."

Kim said, "That boy is like a water hose now."

"Kim, dinner table manners, please."

Al lost the conversation in the hall. The boys' door was closed. He reached for the knob out of habit. He felt the cold metal for just a moment. As he registered the illusion and looked down at it, he lost it. The knob clicked back into place.

I moved it.

He heard Hank crying beyond the door. Al forced himself through the wood to the other side. The door rattled on its hinges. Light was filtering into the room through the faded clown curtains. Al stared at the washed out images of the smiling, white faces.

Damn, that's creepy. We need to tear those down.

"Is that you, Daddy?"

Al was startled. He thought the clowns were talking for one insane moment. He looked around and spotted Hank wrapped in his comforter between his bed and side table.

It's me, buddy. I'm here.

"Are you in Heaven, Daddy?"

No, I'm here. I'm right here. I'll always be here.

"Why, Daddy, what do you want me to do?" Hank whispered through the hood of his comforter.

It might help if you stop wetting yourself all the time, Al thought.

Hank slid his head down into the comforter. "Don't tell anyone, Daddy."

Al stared at the heap of blanket. *He can hear my thoughts too. I guess I need a brain to keep my thoughts secret.*

Hank cried. "No, Daddy, don't steal our brains. I'll do whatever you want. Don't be angry."

The door swung open and Doris said, "You have to stop talking to... your father, Hank. He's not here, honey. He's in Heaven now."

"No, he's not," Hank's voice was muffled through the folds of the comforter.

"Don't you dare say that," Doris shouted.

Al turned around and said, *He's right. I'm not in Heaven.*

Al was facing the closed door in the dark bedroom. He looked back and saw the comforter deflated and empty on the floor under the clown nightlight. Hank was on the bed wrapped in the thin fabric of the curtains. Al looked up and saw the exposed windows and the night sky.

What's happening here?

Hank whimpered under the curtains.

* * *

Al was standing in the kitchen again. The fan was turning slowly.

Hank yelled from the living room. "I'm not going. Daddy will be mad."

"Hank, just stop it. Just stop it," Doris yelled.

Al drifted into the living room and found everyone by the open front door. Al felt afraid looking out at the brightness. Mark was kneeling trying to hold Hank's arm as he was pulling away. Doris had her hands on both sides of her face as she looked down at them. She was in a bright sundress. She was beautiful. Tommy and Kim were standing aside in their finest clothes. Hank pulled off his clip-on tie and threw it on the floor.

What's going on here?

"I'm trying, Daddy. Don't be mad," Hank cried.

"Come on, son. It's okay," Mark said as he lifted Hank up in his arms.

Hank beat his fists against Mark's chest.

Put my son down, Al yelled.

"He's angry," Hank yelled looking over Mark's shoulder. "He's going to hurt us. Please, Mark."

Let go of my son, you … vulture.

"He's very mad," Hank bawled into Mark's jacket.

"I'll protect you," Mark said.

"He just wet your suit, Mark," Kim said.

"It's okay," Mark said rubbing Hank's back. "Everything will be okay."

Hank laid his head down on Mark's shoulder as the man carried him outside. The rest of Al's family followed. Al charged for the door.

"We'll clean up in the car," Mark said. "You can wear shorts at the ceremony, buddy."

"The ring is in these pants," Hank said.

"We'll get it out," Doris put her hand on Mark's shoulder as she pulled the door closed behind them.

"What's a vulture?" Hank asked on the other side of the door.

Al slammed into the door as he tried to go through it. The wood shook in the frame, but did not give. Al moved around to the front window. Hank was already in shorts. His hair was longer. Mark was in a t-shirt and shorts too. He threw the ball past Hank and it rolled toward the street.

Stop him, Al said.

Mark watched as Hank chased the ball to the edge of the yard.

Stop him, Al yelled.

He reached out for the glass, but felt it refuse to allow him through. He pressed with more intensity. The panes in front of him shattered out into the hedges.

Stop, Hank, before you get killed.

"Oh my God," Kim yelled behind Al.

"Did they hit the window?" Doris called from the kitchen.

Al started to turn, but spotted Mark and Hank looking at the broken window. Hank was holding the ball by the curb. His shorts were wet and it was running down his leg. The ball rolled over his quivering fingers and dropped back on the grass.

"He's angry," Hank whispered.

Mark looked at Hank, looked at the window, and then back at Hank. He dropped his baseball glove on the grass. Mark walked toward Hank across the yard.

"It's okay, son. I won't let anything hurt you."

He's not your son. You're not taking him away from me. I'll protect him. I'll do it.

Al stared at the restored window and the empty yard.

Al found himself standing in the dark kitchen. The fan was still. Al listened, but heard nothing.

It must be night, Al thought as he looked at the light coming in from the living room. The window was dirty, but without curtains the sunlight was sharp from the front of the house.

He looked around the kitchen. The microwave, toaster, and refrigerator were gone. Copper tubes twisted up from the dirty floor in place of the missing fridge. Al walked to the counter and looked at the toaster cover lying flat and empty. He reached down, but could not feel it.

Al rounded the counter, climbed the stairs, and approached the door from the hall. The master bedroom was open and empty. There was a stencil on the wall above where the bed had been. It had *Doris & Mark* inside swirling black ribbons and the dark outlines of hearts and flowers.

Lovely ... you know that lowers the resell value.

He walked through the door into the boys' room. The closet was open. There were a few wire hangers on the rack. The room was four walls and a carpet. Everything else was gone except for the old, clown curtains wadded in the corner.

Al turned and approached the door again. The midday light from the exposed windows revealed the hash marks on the doorframe. Al lowered down, level with the marks, and read the dates on each line for Tommy and Hank. When he finished, he read them again.

They are my family, Al whispered, *my family*.

He read the measurements again.

Al found himself in the dark kitchen. He stared up at the sagging blades of the fan. He reached for the toaster cover on the counter. The edges had been chewed by something.

This was my mother's. It belongs to our family.

He couldn't feel it. Al walked through the counter and approached the stairs again. He looked at the broad cracks in the walls as he climbed one step at a time.

If I have to claw through the paint, I'm going to scrape that stencil off the wall, he thought. *It will never resell like that. This is my house and my family. I'm going to be the one that takes care of things.*

A FITTING TRIBUTE
Andrea Janes

———————•◆•———————

By the time she came to live with us, Aunt Anne was already dying.

I watched as her dark carriage rode up to the house, slick and wet in the rain. Papa was anxious and told the servants to draw her a hot bath immediately. I know he fretted because her illness reminded him of my poor consumptive mother. But she was not my mother and this was not her house. She was an interloper intruding on the kingdom I had built with Papa in our city by the sea. I was just a little girl when we sailed here from France. "This all belongs to you now," Papa told me that day when our ship cut through the glittering harbor. The shining rivers were mine, the tall brick buildings were mine, the shimmering church spires towering above everything were mine, too, but most of all, our house was mine.

And now this intruder had come.

I sat in my dressing room the night she arrived, brushing my hair and listening to her. She'd been given the set of rooms next to mine—a large bedroom, a sitting room, and a bath. The dressing room adjoined our suites in the middle. I could hear her, could hear the water splash as she got out of the tub, hear her walk toward the dressing room.

She seemed startled to see me sitting there. "Didn't you expect to be sharing your suite?" I asked coolly, staring at her in the large mirror as I worked the brush through my hair.

I held the hand mirror at an angle to see the back of my head. My hair was thick and black and glossy, curling into lush, deep waves. She watched me scrutinize myself in the vertex of the two mirrors and said, "What a vain child you are."

"I think it would be vainer still to have a maid do my coiffure. To be fussed over."

"And now instead of a maid you have an old aunt." She took my silver brush and began to work it through my hair slowly but without gentleness. "How lucky you are to have such fine hair," she said, fixing her gaze on me.

Her eyes were large and wide-set, almost bulbous, pale green-gray and watery. The ridge of her nose was curved and sharp, her skin waxy. She had a face like a Hapsburg with that weak, turtle-like chin, crooked teeth, and string-bean mouth. How she could be related to me by blood I did not understand.

She caught me looking at her just as my eyes were roving over the great expanse of her forehead. Armies could do battle on that forehead; there was room enough. Perhaps I giggled or smirked because suddenly she looked very cross.

"You know, you won't be sixteen forever," she said, glaring at me, "When you become my age, you will awake one day to find your beauty gone. It will never return."

And with that she pulled off her wig.

At dinner that night I hardly said anything. Anne spoke of all her friends back in Paris, the Chatillons and who-knows-else, and Papa listened ardently. I sat there trying to banish from my mind the image of those dry patches of colorless hair clinging to her lumpy, denuded skull and trying not to laugh.

After dinner, as she and Papa sat downstairs by the fire drinking brandy, I crept into her room. My, but she had a lot of clothing! Dozens of dresses, forests of furs, and hats, of course—hundreds. But what really amused me were the wigs. She had them on funny little heads, combed out or piled high in various styles, all the same shade of brown—as if she was fooling anyone!

The next day I paid a visit to the shop where I often bought costumes for my dance recitals. They were specialists in period dress and accessories, and I found just the thing for dear, dear Aunt Anne.

I could hardly wait until four o'clock when the delivery would come. I tried to read but kept jumping up and looking out the window. Aunt Anne glanced at me from where she was stationed by the fire under her fur blanket—that ridiculous fur blanket!—no doubt to evoke Papa's sympathies to greater effect, and snapped, "What are you so excited about?"

The bell rang, and moments later a servant appeared with a large box. "For you madame." She placed it in Aunt Anne's lap.

"Oh, a gift!" I exclaimed. "Have you got a young admirer?"

She glared at me and opened the box—pulling out an enormous white-powdered wig in the style of Louis XIV.

I laughed so hard, I was on the ground in tears.

Now, Aunt Anne also liked to play the flute. This was her great passion. (At least something was touching those lips of hers!) When she played on warm afternoons, my girlfriends and I would often dance under her window, howling up at her, "Oh play, play! Charm us with your ancient pagan sounds, O goddess of love!" This brought us great amusement, though one day Papa caught us and punished me.

"How dare you mock a sick woman!" he thundered. He sent my friends home and sent me to my room where I sat and laughed to myself, playing the episode over in my mind. What fun a girl could have with a humorless spinster aunt!

That evening she struck back—in her own unimaginative way. I went into my powder room to find my favorite bottle of perfume missing. It was a delicate, orange-scented concoction they called Florida-water in those days, and I wore it always. I suppose she thought the game was on, but I ignored her. The next night my combs and hand-mirror were gone, and the third sunset found the bristles of my hairbrush burned to ash. Next, she had the servants remove the mirror over my dressing table.

Now, I felt that she was becoming less amusing and more of an irritant. I grew tired of playing with my little mouse of an auntie and decided it was time she go.

I made up my mind how to do it. I had no small talent for drawing, and I applied myself industriously to this endeavor most evenings. I began to spend several hours at a time in my study, working away quietly, sketching and drafting, designing a lovely and fitting tribute to my beloved aunt.

There was alchemy in my work. With every line I drew, I dreamed of the day she would die, willing her demise into being. With each mark of the pencil, my energy transmuted the lead into a magic spell I wove around us both. This was not the first time I had effected the demise of a competitor. For you see, I was born with a special gift. I don't know how, and I don't know why, but very early on in my life, I noticed something about myself: whatever I wanted, I got. For instance, if I made up my mind that I would get, say, an apple, within hours there would be a fruit peddler at the door. If I wanted to dance the lead in *Giselle*, I had simply to think it. If another girl was bothering me in school, it wasn't unlikely that she would soon become very sick and be forced to spend the rest of the term in the country.

As I grew older, I became more artful. It wasn't just about wanting things and getting them. It was, rather, a game I played with the universe. This particular game, I decided, was going to be won with grace and style. What's more, this one would create an eternal monument to my art.

The night my drawing was finished, I dressed slowly, leisurely, and wore my hair loose, streaming down in dark waves. I pinned the forelocks back with garnet and amethyst combs, admiring the way they brought out my eyes. The face is the picture, they say, and the hair is the frame.

"Why, my dear," Papa said, "Don't you look lovely." All evening I smiled and chatted and laughed gaily, and Anne sat pale and silent in her seat.

"Aunt Anne has been so quiet tonight," I said after dinner. "Perhaps you'd like to open a gift I made for you. Won't that cheer you up, dear Auntie?"

She opened it, and the room fell silent. There, framed and mounted, was a drawing of her tomb, a monument with the swirling Gothic towers so in fashion right now, with curlicues abounding. Two slender spires flanked an arched canopy within which was a carved bas-relief reading simply "de Cresserons," our surname.

"I've designed it for you, dear Auntie," I said, putting my slim, white arm around her. "As a measure of my devotion."

"You are too kind," she replied, her face ashen. "Excuse me," she said weakly, "I must go to bed."

I smiled at her retreating form and thought, "I win."

Within the week she was dead.

For a while, I felt deliciously unburdened. My world was as it should be, and my home was my own again.

Then one night, about a fortnight after she died, I was just getting into bed when something strange happened. As I pulled the covers up to my chin—for it was a very cold night—something made me gasp. I don't know what it was, nor can I recall exactly the order in which things took place, but the end result of it was that I seemed to have breathed in rather too sharply through my mouth. Somehow I felt a strange tickle as though a bit of hair or dust were lodged in my throat. Just stuck there, tickling me, making me cough. That in and of itself might not have given me pause, but there was something familiar in the air that did. I smelled the sweet smell of Florida-water and I knew she had not gone.

There were other signs that she was still around.

Not once could I leave my room without returning to find everything in disarray, books and papers strewn all about. My clothing was found scissored into slivers. One morning all of my perfume bottles were smashed at once right in front of me; one of the shards cut me.

One night, as I lay in bed unsleeping, I heard the most indescribable noise pervading my room. Try as I might, I could not guess what it was; I only knew that it was Anne, and she was playing another game with me. The best I can say is that it sounded like a shuffling noise, like cloth being brushed and folded perhaps, or, more accurately, dragged across the floor. Curiosity triumphed over fear, and I lit my candle.

Her wigs, every one of them, moved across the floor of their own accord. They seemed to dance, so light were their movements, like leaves in the wind. All across my floor they drifted, tangled tumbleweeds of hair executing delicate fouettés. All of a sudden I felt something brush up against my neck—it was the powdered wig, the Louis XIV wig, moving itself against me for all the world like a kitten who wants to be stroked.

There were occurrences in the daytime as well. Clocks would strike at all hours, never corresponding to the time. Once I heard it strike thirty-seven times before the maid snatched it off the wall with a look of terror. "Why did you stop it?" I asked, "I wanted to see how far it could go." She looked at me. "Bah! You're becoming strange." Was I? Perhaps a change was coming over me. I began to wonder if others could see it, if they could tell that I was haunted.

Another night I awoke to hear the sound of footsteps in my room. It was she. I heard her slip across the room in the darkness and come very near to me, thinking I was asleep. I was shocked to hear the sharp silver sound of scissors snipping right next to my ear! My hand flew up to my hair—ragged chunks were missing. The servants and I looked, but we never found any on the floor or blankets or anywhere else.

Soon the servants had stopped coming into our—my—wing of the house at all.

"You wait," I told her. "Soon I shall be rid of you."

For the tomb that I had drawn had finally been built, and I knew that once we—joy of joys!—put my aunt in the stone walls I designed for her and consecrated her tomb, her spirit would leave our house for good.

The eve of her burial arrived at last. I dressed as though for a party, adorning myself with every bauble Papa ever gave me. I gazed at myself in the dressing room mirror: my eyes were bright, and my amethyst combs shone amid glossy curls. I had to arrange them more artfully this time, to hide the locks of hair that were missing. As I dressed, I smelled the Florida-water and saw a white hand in the mirror's reflection, resting gently on my shoulder. Just a hand, nothing more. I slapped it and said, "Tomorrow we bury you," and it disappeared.

I made my way downstairs. Outside was a howling night of snow and hail, but inside was warm and merry, filled with the smells of roast duck and pink bunches of hothouse roses, my favorite flower. I sat down to dinner under Papa's admiring gaze and began to eat daintily.

Without warning, I began to cough. "Excuse me," I said, but I couldn't stop. There was that tickle in my throat again. There was definitely something caught—I coughed again, more violently. Papa stared at me, but I no longer had any choice in the matter. Perhaps not as subtly as I'd have liked, I reached into my mouth and pulled out a long, black, shining hair. My own. He gasped. I looked down at my plate. Gone was the roast duck and, in its place, masses of damp, dark, curling black tresses. The hair lay there like a newborn creature, dark and slick and glistening, covered in slime.

I coughed again and pulled another hair from my mouth, and then another. More and more, not single strands now, but huge hunks that I hacked out nauseatingly. They fell on my plate in wet clumps as I clawed them out of my throat. My body spasmed and I vomited wet, black hair.

Mortified, I ran from the table.

I collapsed in the hall, falling to my knees in a fresh fit of coughing, tearing at my throat as my body spasmed again. "She cannot breathe!" Papa cried out. The servants gathered around and tried to aid me, but there was seemingly no end to the obstruction in my throat ...

She is here again, wafting the sweet scent of Florida-water, pressing her hands against my throat. I cannot slap them away this time. I am too weak; I cannot breathe. I hear her whisper, very close to my ear, "I win."

As darkness descends, I have a vision of a tomb that says "de Cresserons." My last thought before I die is that I will have to share it with her.

THE SECRET OF ECHO COTTAGE
Sue Houghton

———————•◆•———————

"Jason?" Alison called, pulling her dressing gown tighter around her to shield against the cold.

Stepping out onto the dew-soaked lawn in front of Echo Cottage, she called out again, her breath vaporizing in the foggy night air.

"Jason, is that you?"

She cupped a hand to her ear and listened. A fox barked in the distance. How wrong her friends had been when they'd said the English country life wouldn't suit her. Being two miles from the nearest village was bliss as far as Alison was concerned. The only thing to mar the tranquility was the loud, but infrequent, roar of planes overhead. Compared to the noise and pollution of city traffic where they'd lived before, living beneath a flight path was a small sacrifice.

Alison took a deep breath, the damp air burning her nostrils with the musky scent of fresh earth. She looked back towards the house, whose windows were arranged in such a way they appeared to form a smile. No wonder she'd fallen in love with it.

When the real estate agent had first brought them to see the derelict cottage, just outside Meadowridge, she'd asked about its name.

"It used to be a coaching inn years back. The Rushes, I think," the agent had said. "It was frequented by your lot when they were stationed around here during the Second World War."

Jason had laughed. "By 'your lot' you mean the Americans."

The agent smiled back. "Sorry, yes. Sometime after the war the property became residential."

"And that's when the owners changed the name to Echo Cottage?"

"Seems that way. I've been told it has something to do with the lay of the land around here. If the conditions are right, you'll hear an echo back if you yell. Try it sometime."

Alison had done so on several occasions while they'd been renovating the place. She'd stood in the middle of the lawn and hollered, but not once had she heard an echo back. Jason said it might have something to do with the atmospherics. "Like a yodel from a mountain top." Except the land was flat for miles around. You could almost see the coast on a clear day.

It wasn't a clear day now, though, it was almost midnight. Jason had promised he'd be home early, but then the hospital where he worked had called to say they'd had an emergency and they needed him.

"Tonight of all nights when we have something to celebrate," Alison whispered and circled a hand over her slightly swollen belly. Almost four months pregnant and she hadn't had a clue until she'd taken the test that morning.

She was about to go back inside to try ringing Jason again when a figure appeared from around the side of the cottage.

"Oh, there you are, you startled me," Alison said.

Strange, she hadn't heard his car pull up. It usually made a crunching noise on the gravel. Must be the fog dampening the sound, she thought.

"The dinner's ruined," she said. "It'll be a cheese sandwich if you're lucky. I haven't had a chance to go into the village for groceri ... Ouch!" She lost her footing and stooped to retrieve her slipper. When she looked up there was no one there.

"Jason?"

The light coming from within the cottage wasn't enough to illuminate the area clearly. Had she been mistaken? Gingerly, she started off along the gravel patio, hugging the cottage walls as she did so and cursing herself for not having picked up a flashlight before venturing outside. Something furry scurried across her path and she wondered if some sort of protection might have been a good idea. She stooped to pick up a log from the woodpile, unsure if she had the courage to use it in defense.

As she rounded the side of the cottage, she saw a shadowy figure cross towards the old stables, which Jason was planning to convert to a garage at some stage. At the moment it was filled with debris from remodeling the cottage.

"For heaven's sake, Jason," she shouted, quickening her step to catch up with him. "Didn't you hear me call? You gave me the fright of my life. Hurry up inside."

He stopped and turned to face her. She couldn't make out his features and he didn't answer, just beckoned to her.

"Jason, this isn't funny." Slowly, she inched her way towards the stables. Then she stopped. Wasn't the figure too tall to be Jason? Even so, she felt compelled to follow; her heartbeat throbbed in her temple, and her palms were sweaty with the effort of clutching her makeshift weapon.

As she reached the stable door, she could hear water splashing. Alison knew there was a water butt next to the drainpipe leading from the roof but it was almost empty. Besides, it sounded more like running water.

She summoned up all her courage and was about to dash in and challenge whoever it might be when a thunderous roar of engines came from above. As Alison turned her back on the stables, she felt a presence behind her. Suddenly, there was a pressure in her head as if she'd been hit. A savage pain shot through her belly and she stumbled backwards. The last thing she saw was someone standing over her. And it wasn't Jason.

"Alison? Alison? Are you okay?" a faraway voice said.

As her eyelids fluttered open, she was relieved to see Jason smiling down at her. She was no longer outside, but on the sofa in front of a crackling fire. A stool was beside him on which lay a flannel and a bowl of bloodied water.

Alison gripped her stomach. "Oh, no! The baby!"

"Shush, the baby's fine. Trust me, I'm a nurse, remember? The blood's from a tiny head wound," said Jason. "It looks worse than it is. What on earth were you doing out in the garden at this time of night?"

"I thought I heard you come home. But it wasn't you. A man. Tall ... he beckoned for me follow him. And then the plane startled me." She became a little hysterical. "Jason, I think he hit me on the head."

"You fell, darling. Tripped in those silly slippers of yours." He made her a cup of cocoa and stayed with her on the sofa until she grew calmer.

"I'm sorry," said Alison. "I wanted tonight to be special."

"We can have other special nights." He stroked her hair. "Now, try to stay awake for a while."

But Alison's eyelids soon fluttered closed, and she offered no resistance when she felt herself lifted by strong arms and taken upstairs where she was undressed and carefully tucked into their soft bed.

"Love you, honey," he whispered.

She felt him slide in beside her and spoon against her. Alison breathed in his warmth as big arms drew her closer to him. His lips brushed the back of her neck, and he softly hummed a melody until she drifted off into a peaceful sleep.

The sound of a radio and the smell of bacon woke her. She had no idea of the time but the sun was streaming in through the windows. It had to be around mid-morning.

Jason was beside her with a tray of food. She stretched, and rubbed the sleep from her eyes.

"Good morning," he said, setting the tray of food beside her. "A full English breakfast. Bacon's local. Mushrooms, too. Hey, maybe we should keep our own chicks so we can have fresh eggs every morning."

Alison sat up and looked around the room. She wasn't in their bed. She was still on the sofa where Jason had placed her last night. Yet she could have sworn …

"Jason, I'm confused. How did …"

"How did I manage to cook breakfast without setting the kitchen alight?" He laughed. "But seriously, you should try to eat something if only for the baby's sake. I've called the hospital. I'm not going in to work today. We can spend all day getting one of the rooms ready for our new arrival, if you like."

"Yes, that'd be good. Um, where did you sleep last night?"

Jason rotated his right arm and rubbed the back of his neck. "I didn't want to wake you because you looked so comfortable there on the sofa, so I covered you with a throw and I slept on the floor. We really ought to get a new rug. These old oak floorboards are pretty mean on a man's spine."

She smiled up at him. How lucky she was to have found a man like Jason. "You spoil me," she said. "And singing me to sleep last night goes above and beyond."

"Singing? Don't think so. You know me. Couldn't carry a tune in a bucket. Now eat up. I don't tolerate bad patients."

Alison felt the blood drain from her cheeks. Of course Jason wouldn't have sung her to sleep. He couldn't even sing Happy Birthday in the right key.

"Alison you've gone very pale. Are you in pain?"

She shook her head. "No, it's nothing. I'm being silly. A dream, that's all. Must still be a bit concussed."

"When you're up to it we'll have a run over to the hospital to get you checked over."

"No, I'm fine, honestly."

"I'd rather make sure, and we can grab a bite to eat in Meadowridge afterwards."

"That would be lovely," she said. The smile was a forced one. As he walked away she took in her surroundings again.

"Good news, Alison," said the doctor, after checking her over and examining her scan. "The fall hasn't caused any damage."

"And my injury is consistent with a fall and not being attacked?"

"Alison is convinced someone hit her," Jason explained.

The doctor smiled. "It's my opinion you fell. A bang on the head can be distressing and result in a number of anomalies some of which can manifest as hallucinations, lack of sleep, migraines ..."

"Weird dreams?" asked Alison. "Imagining my husband can sing like Michael Bublé?"

The doctor laughed. "Yes, and all completely normal. A few days rest and you'll be fine."

As they left his office, Jason hugged her. "See, what did I say? Come on, let's eat."

Jason got the drinks in and they sat by the fire at The Mow and studied the lunch menu.

The young woman behind the bar seemed a bit brusque but the landlord pulled up a stool and joined them. He extended a hand to Jason. "Pete. And you'll be the new couple bought Echo Cottage. Jason and Alison, if the rumors are correct."

"That's right," said Jason, "I suppose we can expect to be the subject of village gossip. Foreigners buying up country property, etcetera."

"No, none of that rubbish," Pete laughed and slapped Jason on the back. "You're both very welcome 'round here." He addressed the woman behind the bar. "Aren't they, Belle?"

"Welcome in Meadowridge, yes," she said. "As for welcome at the cottage, that remains to be seen."

"I'm sorry?" said Alison. "Has someone raised an objection to us doing the renovations?"

Belle finished polishing a beer glass before she spoke again. "As I say, that's yet to be seen." She excused herself, saying something about needing to change a barrel in the cellar

"What did she mean?" asked Jason.

"Don't pay her no mind," said Pete. "She's listened to too many tales."

"What sort of tales?" asked Alison.

Pete lowered his voice. "My sister has a vivid imagination. Didn't help that she miscarried a while back. She's been under a lot of stress."

And here we are celebrating our news, thought Alison.

"Listen," said Pete, back to his jovial self. "We're happy someone's doing up the old place at last. Been too long unloved. It'll make a great family home. You settling in okay?"

"Yes, thank you," said Alison. "It's so peaceful. Even with the flight path overhead."

Pete's smile vanished. "Flight path?"

"Yes. The real estate agent was a bit naughty and made no mention of any airport when we first viewed the place. The planes fly right over the cottage. Quite low, in fact, so I'm guessing they must land close by."

Jason was shaking his head. "What planes? I haven't seen any planes."

"Well, you won't have seen them. They pass over during the night," said Alison. "Jason, you must've heard them. There was one last night just before I …" She didn't want to mention her little accident in front of Pete. "Sorry, I must be mistaken. I'm not used to country noises yet."

"Old Charlie Hewitt has been known to take his harvester out all hours," said Pete. "That could explain it. The old boy's one furrow short of an acre, if you get my meaning."

Jason laughed, but Alison didn't.

When Pete got up to serve a customer, she said, "You made me feel really foolish in front of him. I know the difference between the sound of farm machinery and that of a plane."

"Yet you admit you've never actually seen these aircraft."

"You don't believe me, do you?" Alison said, putting on her coat. "Forget the food." As she headed for the door, Jason followed, almost tripping over her when she stopped suddenly to stare at a couple of sepia photographs hanging on the wall. One was of an airfield taken from above; one was of a group of men dressed in American uniform.

She pointed to them and called over to Pete. "Where were these taken?" she asked.

"What? Oh, no idea." He waved a hand dismissively. "Belle's always picking up old photos of the area. Got a bunch of photos of the pub on the back wall, might even be one of your cottage 'round here somewhere."

"When we first came to look at Echo Cottage, the agent said something about Americans billeted around here during the war. Was there an air base, too?"

"Yes." It was Belle who spoke. "In the middle of the Second World War the US military built a runway. Their planes did sorties from there. All top secret. Come the end of the war, they were gone as fast as they arrived. The runway was ploughed up. Put back the way it was."

"Who owns the land now?" Alison pressed.

"Old boy Hewitt. He was only a young lad, ten or so, when the US took it over. His mother died shortly after the war ended. Hewitt didn't inherit it till his father died, but the land has never yielded much. Just enough to keep him from going bankrupt."

Alison was still gazing at the photo. Amongst the group of airmen was someone who looked familiar, but she had no idea why. Tall, blond hair, a look of confidence about him. Dapper would have been the word back then.

And that wasn't all ... right on the edge of the group was a man and a woman. Not in uniform. Not forces, at any rate. They both wore dungarees. Her hair was caught up under a headscarf and she was smiling out at the camera, while he was half-turned towards the other men. No, he was staring directly at the blond airman, a look of pure malice on his face.

Alison felt a sudden wave of nausea and her legs buckled beneath her. Jason caught her before she hit the floor.

"I'm taking you back to the hospital," he said. "That fall last night was worse than I thought."

"It wasn't a fall," she insisted. "I was attacked."

"Not that again. Who could possibly have done that to you?"

She turned to him and stared into his eyes. "That man in the photo. The one standing with the woman in the headscarf. I think it was him who attacked me."

"Now I know you're concussed," he said, walking her to the car.

"That photo was taken over sixty years ago."

"I know, Jason. And incredible as it seems, I recognized the tall blond man in the center." She'd made a note of his name, Flight Lieutenant Carl Parker. "Would you drive me somewhere, please?"

"Where?"

"The Hewitt's place. Maybe the old boy can shed some light. And don't try to talk me out of it."

"I don't intend to. If meeting Hewitt puts a stop to all this nonsense then let's go."

Hewitt looked every bit his age. His unshaven face was lined and weather-baked. And though he at first appeared to be a large man, it became clear when the wind whipped open the old duffle coat he wore, that he wasn't too well fed.

"What do you want?" he growled when Alison and Jason appeared in his yard. "If you're from the Defense, don't waste my time."

"You have a fair bit of land here," began Alison.

Hewitt shook his fist. "It's mine and no 'merican's going to take what's mine."

"One furrow short of an acre, remember," Jason whispered in Alison's ear.

"We're not here to take anything," said Alison, ignoring Jason's remark. "We just wanted to talk to you. We're new to the area, you see. Getting to know the locals."

He eyed them suspiciously. "You're not from t'Agricultural, either?"

"No, honestly," smiled Alison. "Just neighbors, that's all."

He stood looking at them for a moment then turned back towards the farmhouse. "I'll give you five minutes."

The inside of the farmhouse was as rundown as the exterior. Several dogs were curled in front of an old stove. A pine table was littered with newspapers leaving barely enough space for the old man to take his meals. For all the disarray, the coffee percolating on top of the stove smelled amazing, and when Hewitt offered them a mug, they discovered it tasted it, too.

"An Englishman that makes good coffee," joked Jason.

Charlie Hewitt appeared to appreciate the joke, and while Jason engaged him in conversation, Alison was drawn to some photographs on the dresser. They were covered in dust and cobwebs and couldn't have been touched for years except for one, which appeared to have been handled regularly. It was of a slim woman with hair tumbling to her shoulders. She had her face turned away from the camera and her arm linked with someone whose face was in profile.

"Your family?" asked Alison.

"Don't have no family," said Hewitt, without looking at her.

"So who's this?" She picked up the photograph.

Jason obviously felt uncomfortable with Alison's prying. "I'm sorry; my wife gets carried away sometimes."

Hewitt rose and took the photo from her and put it back in its place. "My parents. Long gone. Dad about thirty years or more ago and Ma ... she died in '45, 'mericans killed her."

"The Americans killed her?" A murder? Belle hadn't mentioned that.

Hewitt opened a drawer and took out an album, which he started to thumb through. For a moment it was as though she and Jason weren't even there. Eventually, he snapped the album shut. "So, you've moved into the village. I wasn't aware there was any property up for sale in Meadowridge."

"No, we're a little way out of the village. Echo Cottage. Do you know it?"

Hewitt dropped the album and a photograph spun across the floor towards Alison. She stooped to pick it up, her pulse racing. She stared at an exact copy of the photograph on the wall at The Mow. She compared the man and woman on the periphery to the photograph on the dresser. It was definitely the same couple.

"Your parents seem friendly with the Americans," she said. "There was no animosity over them commandeering their land?"

Hewitt snatched it from her. "Not over the land, no."

"And the tall man in the middle, Lt. Carl Parker, isn't it?"

"You seem to know a lot about my business, young lady."

"I'm sorry, I don't mean to pry. Just curious. Do you know anything about him?"

"Course I does. It were 'im who killed my ma ... good as. Now you've had your five minutes. I've jobs need doin'."

"Did that answer any of your questions?" asked Jason, when they got back in the car.

"I'm not sure yet, but I'm going to find out. We know his mother was killed at the end of the war … about the same time the Americans left …"

"You don't really believe a US pilot murdered Hewitt's mother and got away with it do you?"

"Why not? The whole air base was kept pretty hush-hush so why not a murder? Wait a minute, the person who hit me last night …"

"Alison, please, we've been through all this."

"I know, but humor me for a while. Leaving good sense aside, supposing the person who hit me was Lt. Carl Parker." She tried to bring the image of the man she'd seen standing over her into focus in her mind but it wouldn't come. She shuddered to think he might also have been the man who crooned to her in their bed. The man who'd undressed her and spooned his body against hers.

"You do realize if your theory is right, you're talking about ghosts here?" He rubbed a hand over his face.

Alison knew Jason was fast losing patience with her. If she wanted to investigate she'd have to do it on her own. "You're right," she smiled. "Forget it."

The following day, after Jason had left for his shift, Alison went to the village to find Belle. She eventually caught up with her in the newsagent's.

"Did you know about the Hewitt murder?" Alison asked straight out. If she was banking on shock factor, she was to be disappointed. Belle didn't flinch.

"There was no murder. Why do you want to stir things up? It's all forgotten."

"But not by you? Why are you so interested in what happened?"

"Who said I was?"

"The photographs give it away. Why frame them and hang them on the walls?"

Belle tucked a newspaper into her basket and pushed Alison out of her way. Alison followed her outside onto the street, walking alongside, barely able to keep up with her. Her pregnancy might only be in the early stages but it was making itself felt on her bladder. She wouldn't be able to keep up the pace much longer.

"Damn it, Belle, I know there's something you aren't telling me. Why are you scared?"

Belle turned to face her. "Because I hear the planes too."

Alison could have hugged her. "I knew it! So why is everyone else denying it? Including my own husband."

"Because they don't hear them. Neither did I until you moved in to the cottage. It's as if you've awoken something."

"And the air base? Where's it hidden?"

Belle's demeanor softened towards Alison. "There isn't one. I'd know. I was born 'round here. In the sixties, I grant you, but I do know the last time a plane took off from anywhere close by was 1945."

"So what you're saying is," Alison shivered. "The planes we're both hearing are ..."

Belle nodded. "Echoes from the past."

Alison invited Belle over to the cottage that afternoon and was thrilled when she accepted. "Echoes from the past," said Alison, through the steam on her coffee. "Makes sense of the cottage's name now. Other than the planes, has anyone ever actually seen anything?"

"Ghosts? Sure."

Alison's eyes widened. "The airman? Have people seen him?"

"They thought so, but on investigation, it turned out to be old boy Hewitt traipsing 'round his fields at midnight. Drunk as a skunk, often as not. And when he wasn't sitting in the top field talking to the haystacks, he was plowing it up for no good reason."

"Maybe looking for something? His mother's body, what happened to it?"

Belle laughed. "Buried in the village churchyard, where else? And I told you, Ruth Hewitt wasn't murdered. Only old boy Hewitt believes that. Her death was attributed to a hemorrhage."

"A brain hemorrhage? How awful. And so young."

"No, it was a uterine bleed. Maybe a tumor, who knows. Trouble was, the village doctor had been conscripted at the start of the war. Seems it was some old quack from the nearest town dealt with her."

At that moment, Alison felt her baby move for the first time. She placed her hand on her belly. A powerful feeling of love overwhelmed her. Something else moved her too. "How do you know the cause of Hewitt's mother's death?"

"Looked it up in the newspaper archives. You aren't the only one with an inquisitive mind."

"So we still don't know what Hewitt was looking for, or why there are ghosts around the stables." She sighed. "I just wish we had more on

Ruth Hewitt."

Belle blushed. "Actually, we have half a letter she wrote to the vicar."

"How'd you find that?"

"Vicar Brown helped me go through the old files they have at St. Bede's. I think he's a bit sweet on me." Her blush deepened before she rushed on, changing the topic back to Ruth Hewitt. "There was a letter she wrote seeking the church's advice on what she calls 'a delicate matter.' Probably a divorce. Most of the letter from thereon is water-damaged and illegible but I get the idea there's something she hid away prior to her death. To be honest it's all rather cryptic. But it may be the thing Hewitt's been looking for all these years."

"I've just had an idea." Alison grabbed a flashlight from a kitchen cupboard, and she and Belle headed towards the stables. Clambering over renovation debris, rusting garden implements and boxes not yet unpacked from their move to England, Alison shone the flashlight into every corner of the building. The musky, dank odor of neglect lay heavy in the air.

"What are we looking for?" asked Belle, batting away curtains of cobwebs.

"I'm not sure. But this is the place Ruth and Carl used to meet, right? So it makes sense that whatever she's hidden is here."

"But it won't just be lying around or someone would have found it by now," Belle said. "It'd have to be hidden."

Alison closed her eyes and tried to recall what she'd heard the night Carl led her to the stables. "Running water," she said. "No, I heard rushing water."

"There's a subterranean stream runs below the house, everyone knows that," said Belle. "That's why the inn was originally called The Rushes."

Yes, Alison vaguely remembered seeing it on the plans when they'd bought the cottage. She leaned against one of the horse troughs and tried to gather her thoughts. "If a river runs beneath the house, it would probably continue below the stables."

Belle picked up a rusty bucket from the trough. "There's a well," she said. "When it was a coaching inn, there'd be a well for bringing water up from the river into the horse troughs."

Belle tapped her boot on the flags. Alison joined her, moving across the stable. Suddenly it sounded hollow beneath Belle's foot. "I think I've found something."

Belle knelt and scraped away layers of dirt from the floor to reveal a circular wooden well cover. They heaved and tugged at its metal latch until, with a crack, the corroded metal snapped, sending them sprawling. "What now?" asked Belle.

Alison rummaged through the pile of old garden implements. "Try this," she said, handing Belle a crowbar.

Belle wedged it under the lip of the well cover and stamped on the other end. It snapped in half, but it had done its job. The cover shot open revealing a deep pit around four feet across.

Alison shone her flashlight into the well. "I can see the water sparkling at the bottom." The only other thing it yielded beside a fishy pong was disappointment.

"You still haven't told me what you expected to find," said Belle.

Alison had her head cocked to one side. "Listen. Can you hear that?"

It grew more distinct until they could hear the words, too. It was the same tune Alison heard the night when she'd been put to bed ... or imagined she had. She now knew it'd been Carl's spirit comforting her.

'*Don't sit under the apple tree with anyone else but me ... anyone else but me...*'

Alison looked towards the stable doors. A man in uniform was standing behind a woman, her dungarees and headscarf clearly visible even though she was in silhouette with the light behind her. Carl and Ruth. Ruth raised a hand and pointed directly at the well. In a breath they were gone.

Alison knew then that they were looking in the right place. "Belle, look again. It has to be here."

Belle obliged and lay flat on her belly and stuck her arm into the well. "There's a ledge here," she said, exploring the rocky surface with her fingers. "Just under the lip." She used the broken crowbar to scrape away loose rubble, sending it splashing into the water below. Suddenly she stopped. "I think I've found something."

Alison, mindful of her condition, knelt beside Belle and helped her bring the find to the surface. It was a small vanity case, filthy with mildew. Part of the metal clasp had long since rusted and fallen away. A few more years and it would've disintegrated and its contents been lost forever.

"What's in it do you think?" asked Belle. But the look on her face said she'd guessed.

With trembling hands, Alison opened the case. Tiny bones, wrapped in the remains of a crocheted, pink blanket lay inside.

* * *

The forensics report estimated the infant had been almost full term.

Charlie Hewitt walked into the local police station the day after the baby was found and made a confession.

"To think the poor man had carried the guilt with him all those years," said Alison to Jason as she cuddled their baby son several months later. "Not that it was his fault. He was only a child when his father sent him to spy on his mother."

Apparently, Seth Hewitt, a beast of a man, had made Charlie follow his mother to Echo Cottage, or The Rushes, as it was then called, where he saw her in the stables, in the arms of Lt. Carl Parker. He heard talk of a baby, Carl's baby. Carl was going to take them to America with him now that the war was all but over. Charlie wrongly thought he was to be left behind at the mercy of his evil father, so, in childish pique, he reported everything back to him. When his mother returned home that night, Seth Hewit had flown into a rage and delivered her a savage beating.

"Ruth must've been terrified," said Alison. "Keeping the pregnancy from her husband all those months and then to escape the house after such abuse and make it to the stables only to give birth to a stillborn child, alone." Alison shuddered.

"I doubt she knew she was dying," said Jason. "I think she fully expected Carl to come to their rescue, but Carl was killed that same night in his last sortie from the airbase."

Alison never mentioned it, but she was sure it was Carl who carried her upstairs and held her close the night she'd been injured. He was taking care of her baby, as he'd been unable to do for his lover's.

By the time Ruth was found the next day she'd hemorrhaged to death. Charlie had since confirmed to police that he knew his father had bribed the locum doctor to falsify the death certificate.

Jason stroked his baby's head. "Seth Hewitt must've thought the baby had gone into the well and been lost to the river. A very tidy outcome for him."

"Or so he thought. He'd never know that Ruth hid the baby's body in one last act of defiance. And she's waited all these years for someone to discover the baby and return her to her arms."

Charlie Hewitt went back to his farm after all the media coverage died down. He no longer blamed the American airman for his mother's death. Nor did he plough up his fields in the middle of the night when he was worse for wear.

Alison never heard the planes again. But sometimes, when the moon cast a shadow across the lawns of Echo Cottage, Alison imagined she could see two lovers embracing, a child in their arms. And a melody echoing softly in the trees.

'Don't sit under the apple tree with anyone else but me ...'

COOTER, ASS-MUNCH, AND ME
Calie Voorhis

Go ahead and sit down anywhere, honey. There's plenty of empty seats—all of them, in fact. What will you have? We've got Guinness, Harp, and Coors Lite on tap. A Guinness? Coming right up.

So, you're the reporter lady wants to hear about Cooter. No, I don't mind if you use a recorder. Just to let you know though, electronic objects don't always get along with me so much. You'd be better off with paper, but it's up to you, of course.

It wasn't my idea, to name the ghost Cooter, any more than Ass-munch lying there in the corner behind the bar licking his balls is my dog. Yeah, you saw me giving him some water and half my sandwich. Dog's gotta eat, after all.

No, John the owner held a contest and all the regulars chipped in with suggestions for the name. John thought it would add "ambiance." It bugs me he can't even pronounce the word properly. Me, I try to pay attention to the way things are pronounced. Helps me fit in.

"If we got on the ghost tour, I'd bet we'd get some more regulars," John said. "All we gotta do is make up the ghost."

It was a busy night, so while John blathered on about wanting a proper Confederate ghost for a proper southern bar, I maneuvered around him pouring drinks.

What's that? Oh yes, it's a bit cramped down here. The place feels closed in to me as well. Low ceiling, stone walls, and we're pretty much all the way underground. Almost claustrophobic when it gets crowded, but I don't mind so much as long as I'm behind the bar and the drunks are on the other side.

Anyways, stupid idea, I thought, but didn't say. He's my boss after all, ya know? Not the first one I've had here, nor probably the last, but he's the current one.

No locals go on the ghost tour; it's only the out-of-towners who gawk at the gingerbread houses, obediently trailing behind the pirate-dressed guide, like ducklings following their mother. And tourists, as any bartender in this town'll tell ya, tip fer shit.

So you see, it's clearly John's fault for the trouble we're in now.

It was also his idea to adopt the dog.

"Come on," he said. "We'll have a bar dog. A mascot. Chicks will dig it."

John always was one for anything that might bring in the chicks, the closer to twenty-one the better for him. I guess he likes 'em naïve. At that age, they still think owning a bar is really something, even if it does only hold forty-four people according to the Fire Marshall's occupancy certificate. I guess he thinks it makes up for the paunch he tries to suck in and his comb-over.

Me? Oh, I like them older, if at all. But the kind of older women who come into a place like this are either tourists, not knowing any better and liable to leave town as soon as you get to know them, or regulars. I can't date a regular. It'd be like a shrink dating his own patient. You know, for a bartender like me to see a regular. And no offense meant to you, but white women ain't my style. I like chocolate—as they say these days. Someone with skin color same as mine. I haven't offended you, have I? We can't help our tastes, you know?

You want another? Hold on a sec and I'll start the pour. Have to let Guinness settle properly, ya know. I like a lady who drinks Guinness, by the way.

Well, anyhow, he went out and found this poor black lab mutt with a crooked tail and brought him back. His butt was so flea-eaten it looked you could see them hopping about—all the fur had come off and scarring'd left the skin shiny and pink underneath. The first time he saw me his eyes went all big and he started howling and whining. He's gotten used to me now though, and me him.

So let me ask you—who do you think takes care of the darned dog? Who do you think lets him out of the bar to do his business in the lone bush out front? Me, that's who.

Let me get back to the ghost though. Ass-munch is only incidental to the story, really, though he was the first one to see him.

I do have to say, after John decided to invent the ghost, it did provide entertainment for quite a few nights while we worked the whole thing up.

Norm was the one who, Southern stock that he's from, decided he had to be the ghost of a Confederate soldier.

Julie decided he'd dropped dead in this very bar.

Mary Taylor added the bartender had poisoned him because of a love triangle. She's a real hoot, that lady. Bitter and mean. I think she mighta poisoned one of her husbands, but who can keep track of them?

At that point I put in my two cents. "Ain't scary enough," I told them. "Besides," I said, "I don't want a story going around about a bartender poisoning customers. Ain't good for business. Why not a ghost story about a slave?"

Here, let me get you a coaster for your beer. You're a real good listener, ya know? Kinda funny—supposed to be the bartender doing the listening. But I guess you writers also know how to listen.

But nope, their hearts were set on having a Wilmington Confederate ghost. Me, I think the South gets too hung up in all that stuff, especially considering all the other things that've happened in this town. Why, you know we were responsible for the first act of rebellion in the British Colonies? See, I knew you didn't. No one does.

So anyways, they ended up with their Confederate ghost and decided after much deliberation he'd've been a young man. Handsome, of course. White, of course. Born to a well-to-do family from right here in town. Hearing the call of glory and service to his country, and in honor of southern womanhood yada yada, he marched off to war. During these years, he covered himself in glory, until finally the South was defeated by them dreaded Yankees. Injured, he crept back to his hometown and hid himself in this here bar, only it was a cache used by the blockade runners back then.

His sister, a gentle soul, brought him food and tended to him when she could, for the northern occupiers were settled in town and the once-proud families were reduced to being little more than servants in their own houses.

Personally, I think it served the stubborn sods right. I'm just surprised the slaves didn't burn the places down around them before they left. I sure as shit would've.

Let me pour you another. Naw, put your money away—this one's on me. I don't get much business these days.

Hey, Ass-munch! Stop it!

That dog would chew hisself all day long if I let him.

Winter came cold as can be that year. So cold even the oak trees lost their leaves and the palms all up and died. Well, fever came on their house. Still, Catherine (or at least that's what I call her) nursed her parents day and night, leaving their side only to tend to her brother, sneaking through the old sewers into what's now the bathroom.

Oh yeah—there're really tunnels here. Blocked up of course. Some people will tell you they're part of the Underground Railroad, but that's a bunch of horseshit, if you'll pardon my French. They're old sewers from the days when they just let it all flow into the river. Still, I bet slaves took advantage of them to run away. Wouldn't you? And I bet a few of the poor sods died in here—found themselves trapped in the water and came in here for shelter only to find it all locked up. Bet they tried to dig themselves out. Just like the Confederate who never existed.

Well, you don't care about that—you want Cooter's story.

Of course her parents died and Catherine contracted the fever herself. She died before she could share her secret with anyone, and her brother died too, of hunger and thirst, surrounded by the storage pile of the guns of the demolished Confederate army. You see, she'd locked him in to make sure he was safe and didn't wander in his fever.

This is the point where you're supposed to shiver with the terror of the thought of being locked up here in the dark, swooning with fever, waiting day after day in the close confines for a sister who never comes.

And this is where I do my spooky voice. "They say, after dark on winter nights, he roams this here bar trying to get out with hands all a bloody from digging, screaming in the dark for someone to come save him."

Relax, ma'am. Yeah, the lights going off almost made me scream, too. Guess the story made you a little jumpy. Here, let me light a couple of candles. The electricity goes out sometimes. No particular reason at all. Cause the building's old or a tree swaying on a power line somewhere.

Don't worry though, none of the story's real. Like I said, we all made it up. John went and told it to one of the tour guides, and I guess she must've told it to another. You know how these things get spread.

So here we had this great story. Only the ghost didn't have a name and it made John feel a little sorry for him, if you can imagine it. Feeling sorry for a nonexistent ghost. Humph. But it was only after all the stories we told each other when the bar was quiet and all, that he started to feel a little real to us perhaps.

So we held a contest. Five dollars to enter, with the money going to the boys' and girls' clubs.

You're still recording this, right? You said you wanted to hear the true story behind Cooter and this is it, even if it ain't as much fun as the tales you heard.

Ass-munch, I swear if you don't stop your gnawing I'm going to put you back out on the streets!

Yeah, I give him beer sometimes. Don't look at me like that. He's a big dog. A little dish won't hurt him none and it stops him chewing on hisself for a bit. Can't stand that awful slurping sound.

I think it was Mary Taylor put in the name Cooter. Before I knew it, there was a campaign on and normal names like "Patrick," or "Henry," or "Jebadiah," were out. Instead we got "Billy Bob." And "Bubba" of course. For a while "Enus" was right up there in the running.

No, I don't hear anything dripping. But it's probably just that faucet in back. I'll check it later, ma'am.

Of course, Cooter won out. What a thing! To name the ghost of a proper, Southern gentleman after a snapping turtle. Course, Cooter has other meanings, too, ya know?

Oh, you're from up North? Yeah, well around here, Cooter can refer to a part of a lady's anatomy. Oh, don't blush—I ain't gonna name the specific part, you being a lady and all.

Strangest thing though. Even though they knew we made the story up, freaky things started to happen.

Did I ever see him? Nope, but Mary Taylor swears she did. 'Course, Mary Taylor drinks a bit more than is good for her. It wouldn't surprise me none if she saw a dragon flying through the sky on a clear blue day. She said he was a handsome man with a big mustache and spotless gray uniform, buttoned up at the throat. Which is a downright lie—the Confederates weren't in any sort of shape by the end of the war. And I should know.

Bottles jumped off the shelf and worse. Patron's glasses emptied soon as they turned their back on the bar. The toilets kept stopping up. The sump pump would quit overnight and the bar would be two inches deep in water by morning.

Oh yeah, the ghost tours came but they never stayed long, just long enough for the guide to tell the story. People told me they could smell something rotting, like a dead possum.

You smell it too? I guess I must be used to it. Don't smell any different than it ever has to me.

Oh, I've been here for years and years now. Can't even really remember. That's how long it's been. Some say I came with the bar!

The regulars all stopped coming. Oh, no, not all at once. Wasn't like they sat down and made a decision to move on. Just gradually over time they stopped dropping by. The ghost tour stopped coming too. Said for John to call them when he got rid of that horrible smell—said the tourists didn't want to smell dead things.

Me, I think something got mad. Something that weren't no Confederate soldier. Something that would've been ashamed and angry at even being thought Confederate. Something, well, I guess I should say, someone, who thought Cooter was a downright ridiculous name. I think he decided he didn't want any more of it and maybe he'd just drive them all away until the story faded out. Don't seem to be any signs of it happening yet, though, if you're here.

What's that? On the bar top? Yeah, that's blood.

It's just my palms bleeding. Happens every once in a while. I was hoping you wouldn't notice.

Well, that tears it, Ass-munch, she's gone. Damn, but I sure wish I hadn't tried to escape through the sewers. Seemed like a good idea at the time. Maybe they'll stop calling me Cooter soon.

HUNGRY FOR ONE MORE HAUNTING?

Check out

The Haunted Housewives of Allister, Alabama
by Susan Abel Sullivan

"A writer blessed with imagination and wit."
— Hugo Award Winner Allen Steele

Coming October 2012

from World Weaver Press

*Turn the page to read the opening chapter and pick up the full novel
when it comes out in print on October 30, 2012,
or grab the early-release ebook on October 16, 2012!*

CHAPTER ONE
Late September

1

My name is Cleopatra Kilgore Tidwell. As a middle class Southern gal born and raised in small town Alabama, I was brought up with certain social rules. You don't wear white after Labor Day, you don't decorate your lawn with pink flamingos, and you most certainly don't hang black velvet paintings in your home.

So when my husband Bertram and I were recruited to help his mother pare down her Elvis collection and pack up the rest of her stuff for her upcoming move to a senior's condo, I was a bit judgmental about all the tacky Elvis doo-dads.

Okay, I was a good bit judgmental. Don't get me wrong. Out of the three mothers-in-law I've had, Georgia is hands down my favorite. But really? A black velvet painting of Elvis Presley? That was "supposedly" haunted. She might as well have hung a dogs-playing-poker print smack dab in the middle of her living room. It was just not done in Allister unless you were a redneck or trailer trash.

And Georgia was neither, bless her heart.

My mother, Martha Jane, always says, "Hindsight is wiser." I didn't know at the time that the "haunted" Velvet Elvis would lead to murder, mayhem and a media circus. Or that my whole worldview on the subject of psychics, angels, the occult, and disembodied spirits would be turned on its head. Yep, I was in for a rude awakening. Uh huh.

2

My gorgeous mother-in-law, who at sixty-two could still turn younger men's heads, plucked a framed 8x10 photograph from the end table beside her couch. Her spacious ranch home was in complete disarray from the three of us sorting through a lifetime of belongings for her upcoming move to a smaller abode. But Georgia herself was the epitome of neatness, her blonde hair done up in a 60s flip, her navy slacks neatly pressed, and not a smudge of dirt or dust on her hot pink knit top.

"Oh, Bertram, I absolutely must take this photo to the condo with me."

"Now, Mama, you know you can't take everything with you."

Bertram stroked his beard, a clear sign he was thinking up some alternative for his mother. He'd opted against his usual suburban uniform of khakis and polo shirt and was wearing jeans and a Jimmy Buffet t-shirt touting the song, "It's Five O'Clock Somewhere."

"How about you trade something in your gonna-keep pile with that photograph?" He rose to his full six foot four height, his knees cracking with the effort. He pointed to the spot on the golden shag carpet where we'd gathered a growing pile of Elvis memorabilia. "Like this Velvet Elvis?"

He hoisted up a two by three foot acrylic painting of Elvis preserved for all posterity on black velvet and bordered with a gold frame that would have been right at home in a Liberace museum. This was the often parodied Elvis: white rhinestone-spangled jumpsuit, chiffon scarf, dark, longish hair in the early seventies style, thick mutton-chop sideburns, and a hint of a jowl. For an odd moment, I thought I heard Elvis saying, "Priscilla," in my head. And then it was gone.

"But that's the painting I bought last month when I went to Graceland," Georgia said. "A little fella was sellin' 'em by the roadside. Said it was haunted. I paid a thousand dollars for it."

Oh, Lordy, Martha Jane would be fit to be tied if she heard this. A thousand dollars for something only a bonafide Elvis fanatic would want and hideously tacky, to boot.

Bertram frowned. "A thousand dollars, Mama?" He was still holding the painting, staring at Elvis's one eye as if he could silently discern its dubious secrets. I was just relieved the trashy thing didn't belong to us.

"Well, yes, hon. If this was the real deal, I wanted to be the next person to witness it. I wasn't about to let another Elvis collector get their hands on it." She nodded at me as if I were a kindred spirit.

"How is it haunted?" I'm tellin' ya, some people will believe anything.

"Well, the little fella said it sang 'Heartbreak Hotel' at night after he and his family had all gone to sleep. A pitiful soul. He reminded me of those men you see by the interstate holding up the will-work-for-food signs."

Bertram set the painting down on the thick carpet again, propping it against the wall, but one hand lingered along the upper edge of the gilt frame. "If they were all asleep, how'd they know it sang anything?"

"Because he videotaped it. And he also told me it showed Elvis leavin' the painting."

I didn't doubt for one moment that this was all a gimmick to dupe the gullible, but it could be entertaining to see someone's amateur efforts at pulling a con. "Did he give you the tape?"

"No, darlin'," Georgia shook her head sadly. "Said it burned up in a trailer fire."

It was on the tip of my tongue to say, "Yep, sure it did." But I kept my mouth closed. Martha Jane used to say, "If you can't say something nice, don't say anything at all." Not that that ever stopped her.

Bertram couldn't seem to keep his hands off the painting's gold frame. "Which one is more important to you, Mama? The signed photograph or the haunted painting?"

Georgia sighed. "I guess I'll keep the photograph. I'd truly hoped I'd get to commune with Elvis's dearly departed spirit, but nothing's happened so far. Maybe someone else'll have better luck with it."

Bertram hefted the thing, his biceps bulging. "Then I'll just set it over here in the gotta-go pile."

For a medium-sized painting, it seemed to weigh a lot.

Georgia hugged the photograph to her bosom. "Cleo, honey. Set down what you're doin' and come take a look at this."

I was happy to oblige. We'd been at it for awhile and I was ready for a break. I had no idea one person could accumulate so much stuff, most of it Elvis related.

She passed me the old black and white photograph. It was from the early sixties. Georgia, Elvis Presley, and a lanky, blond mystery man posed together in front of a swimming pool surrounded by lush, tropical plants. Georgia was in the middle, the guys on either side of her, their arms draped across one another. The three of them looked pretty chummy together. Georgia reminded me of Connie Stevens and Sandra

Dee with a little Doris Day thrown in, the all-American girl. Elvis was young and still beautiful.

The King's scrawl jittered across the bottom half of the photograph.

Georgia.
We certainly had fun in Acapulco.
Yours, Elvis

I pointed to the mystery man. "Who's this?"

"Oh, that's Lee Munford. He was part of Elvis's Hollywood entourage. He and Elvis would stay up late talking about the occult and life after death."

Good to know. Like that bit of trivia would ever come in handy. Uh huh.

Georgia was not to be deterred from trying to take it all with her.

"Bertram, hon, it's so hard to choose which things to keep and which to let go. Are you sure you two can't store some of these in that roomy Victorian Cleo just inherited?" She gestured grandly like Vanna White on *The Wheel of Fortune*, indicating enough Elvis memorabilia to stock a Graceland gift shop.

Say no, say no, say no, I thought, mentally crossing my fingers. My great-aunt Trudy, who left us her house a few months ago when she died at the ripe old age of ninety-nine, would roll over in her grave if she knew we might use it to store Elvis crap. Elvis had been a vulgar upstart in her way of thinking.

"Mama, we've been over that. Cleo and I have nothing against the King, but we're just not into him like you are."

Whew! Actually, we weren't into him at all. I could rattle off a laundry list of Elvis aversions that Bertram had from growing up with an Elvis nut for a mother. Trust me, it was enough to put anyone off Elvis for life.

Georgia lovingly wrapped the picture in white paper. "Cleo, did I ever tell you that Elvis dyed his hair? He was actually a natural blond. Or that his middle name was Aaron?"

"Why yes, Georgia," I said as sweetly as I could, "I believe you did." *Several times.*

For a moment she had a startled, expression. I'd probably derailed her entire thought process. But she recovered quickly and said, "So how are you two love birds celebrating your third anniversary?"

Bertram and I exchanged knowing glances, favoring each other with a little smile. I shrugged and said, "We're spending a quiet evening home alone. Nothing fancy."

Nothing fancy! We were only going to celebrate the Super Bowl of Romance in our new home. Married three years and we still had the heat of newlyweds.

"Well, that's sweet, hon. I wish you both a lifetime of happiness."

3

Champagne buzzed through me like the soft whirr of cicadas on a hot summer's night. Our third wedding anniversary had been absolutely exquisite up to this point. A candlelight dinner for two in the formal dining room of our new Victorian home. Kansas City steaks, grilled to perfection. Cherries Jubilee and not a single scorch mark on the antique lace tablecloth. Bertram: looking absolutely yummy in a charcoal gray suit. And me all gussied up in a slinky red dress, my blonde hair curled and pinned up off my neck. We'd broken out the good china, silver, and crystal for the occasion.

Bertram had burned a CD of romantic songs. As he cleared the dessert dishes from the table, "The Way You Look Tonight" segued to Elvis Presley's version of "Can't Help Falling in Love." He must have gotten that one from Georgia since we didn't own any Elvis music. But it was a romantic song. What sort of gift would Bertram give me this year? He'd presented me with a box of Godiva chocolates and the entire set of Maude Adams mysteries on our first anniversary. And tickets to see Jimmy Buffet at the Fox in Atlanta last year. I was aquiver with anticipation.

And then he toted out the Velvet Elvis.

"Happy Anniversary, Cleo."

A laugh bubbled out of me. Oh, what a good one. We'd remember this anniversary for years to come.

"No, really, Cleo," Bertram said, his brown eyes troubled. "Happy Anniversary."

And then it hit me. This *was* my anniversary gift. I stared at 70s Elvis in his white jumpsuit and mutton-chop sideburns, painted so, um ... artistically ... on black velvet, trying to think of something—anything— to say. The only words I could come up with were: *Oh my God*. If I had to make a list of gifts I'd least like to receive, a velvet painting of any kind would be at the top, right above tickets to Muppets on Ice or maybe a ceramic gnome for the front yard. It wasn't so much the hideousness of it as the shock of the unexpected. It was as if I'd been expecting to go to dinner at a five-star restaurant only to be taken to McDonald's for a Happy Meal. And if it had been a gag gift, I could have played along, but this was our wedding anniversary.

The silence was stretching out to an uncomfortable span, accentuated by the ticking of the grandfather clock in the adjacent parlor. I had to say something, and I had to say it now. But I didn't want to hurt Bertram's feelings, not on our special night.

"It's, uh … Bertram, I don't know what to say."

Bertram propped it against the back of one of the gold upholstered dining room chairs, and we admired the thing together. How cozy.

"After we helped Mama move," he said, his arm draped around my shoulder. "I just knew I had to get it. It had *you* written all over it."

"It did?" I was trying so hard to be careful with what I said.

"Yeah. Like neon lights. And you can tell all your friends about it being haunted."

"I can?" I didn't want to tell my friends about it at all. I didn't want to tell *anyone* about it. I think I'd die from embarrassment.

"Sure. You'll be the talk of the town. Who else can say they own a genuine, haunted painting of the King?"

"No one?"

"No one, but you." Bertram gave me a squeeze. Even with high heels on, the top of my head barely reached his chin.

I could hear it now. I'd be the joke around town. *Oh, that Cleo Tidwell, married three times. Her husband gave her a Velvet Elvis on their anniversary. Isn't that the tackiest thing you ever heard?* And then they'd chortle like a pack of hyenas.

But I looked up into my husband's handsome face at that moment, and my bafflement and concern got shoved to the back burner. His brown eyes were so full of love.

So I said, "Thank you, Bertram," standing on tiptoe and throwing my arms around his neck. And even then, he had to lean down to kiss me, his beard tickling my lips. But it was a five-alarm kiss that made my toes—and other parts—tingle. Bertram scooped me up Rhett-Butler-style and carried me up the grand staircase to our boudoir where we scattered a couple of cats off the bed.

The Velvet Elvis couldn't have been farther from my mind.

4

When I came downstairs for breakfast the next morning, all seemed right with the world. I had on my favorite L.L. Bean navy walking shorts, a white scooped-neck knit top, and a pair of navy Keds. My unruly hair was pulled back into a ponytail with a gross grain hairband. My make-up was Cover Girl perfect. And Bertram and I had had a spectacular night in the bedroom.

But what should I find in the formal dining room but my husband of three years balancing on one of Great-aunt Trudy's antique chairs before the fireplace, a hammer cocked in one hand and a nail poised against the cabbage rose wallpaper. And right before he was supposed to head out to work.

Oh, I could just kill him! Those delicate chairs weren't made for a six foot four, two hundred and twenty pound man to stand on them.

"What are you doing?" I said, each word in staccato.

He jerked around to look at me, and I heard a distinctive crack from the chair.

"I know the *perfect* place to hang your painting," he said. "It came to me this morning in the shower."

"In the dining room? Of a Victorian house? Wouldn't it be better in ... that back room upstairs?"

"No," Bertram sang out all cheery, "you'll want this prominently displayed so you can show it off."

And then he pounded the nail home.

Oh. Oh. Oh. I couldn't bear to watch. This *so* went against the social rules I was raised with.

Bertram set the hammer on the mantle and actually scampered across the gleaming hardwood floor to where we'd left the Velvet Elvis the night before. Then he practically traipsed back to the scene of the crime with it. I winced as he stepped upon the antique chair again.

"Bertram, couldn't you have used a step ladder? That chair can't hold your weight. It's fifty years old, for crying out loud."

"No time," he sang out, totally unfazed. He hung the painting, leveled it, and then stepped down to admire his handiwork. "Perfect."

"Uh, Bertram?"

"I also got a great idea for a new half-time show this morning. I don't know why I never thought of it before." Bertram was the Director of Bands for Allister State University and he was much more proficient with a musical instrument than he was with handyman tools.

He left the chair and hammer where they were and disappeared in the direction of the butler's pantry. "We'll do a tribute to Elvis. The alumni will love it."

The things that make you go: *hmmm*. If it hadn't been for the Velvet Elvis, I wouldn't have thought twice about a show dedicated to Elvis.

Bertram breezed out of the pantry into the big open foyer, a Dr. Pepper in one hand and a granola bar in the other. He broke stride only long enough to kiss me on the forehead. "That was some night last night, Cleo. See you at lunch."

As soon as his convertible backed out of the drive, I whisked the step ladder out of the laundry room and climbed up in front of the velvet-offense-against-good-taste. The King still sang silently in profile, rhinestones glittering, microphone held high. I listened, hands poised on either side of the gold frame. Nothing. Nothing but house noises, like the hum of the fridge in the kitchen, and the ticking of the grandfather clock, and a board creaking upstairs from our fat cat Cosmo.

"Darlin', you're comin' down," I told the painting.

It didn't answer. Good thing, too, or I probably would have fallen off the step ladder and sprained something.

I grasped the frame to lift it off the wall, but couldn't get it to budge. Geez, maybe I should have eaten my Wheaties. I tried again. Ergh, the thing was too heavy to move. What was it made out of? Gilded lead?

Maybe I could use my powers of persuasion to convince Bertram to relocate it tonight. In the meantime, I could live with it on the wall. It wasn't like anyone was coming over today, at least not for a social call.

I had just snapped the step ladder closed when the doorbell did its dull ding. Goodness, who could it be so early in the morning?

The who was Marty Millbrook, my second ex-husband. His color scheme would have made the sisters of Phi Mu squeal with joy. Green polo shirt, pink and green plaid shorts, navy belt, and pink slip-on tennis shoes. How many times had I told him that red heads shouldn't wear pink?

"Well, hey, Cleo. I'm glad I caught you at home."

I pulled him inside and gave him a big hug. It's no secret that I still adore Marty. But he's like a second sister ... or a gay brother ... or hell, I don't know. What I do know is we survived our divorce to become great friends.

"You're up and at 'em early this morning."

"Just trying to catch that ole worm." His face lit up with a boyish grin.

Our house is a combination of Victorian and Craftsman design. At one time, the big open arch between the larger parlor and the dining room probably sported a thick velvet drape hung on a rod. The drape could be tied off for roominess or left closed for privacy. But the drape was long gone, and anyone standing at my front door had a clear view of a large portion of the dining room.

Marty now leaned way out to his left, his expression incredulous. "Cleo, that Velvet Elvis in your dining room has got to go. I thought you had better taste than that."

"I do." I gave him the scoop.

"Straight men." He shook his head in sympathy. "But you are a lucky girl in all other ways. That Bertram is quite a catch."

"Yes, isn't he?" I almost purred thinking about all those ways.

"All right, sweetie," Marty said, pulling a folded up piece of paper from his shorts pocket. "I'll get to the point. The Historical Society is having a historic home tour to raise money to buy and restore the old Parnell place on Main Street. We're calling it a Haunted History of Allister. Of course, none of the homes are haunted, but we're modeling it after the one in New Orleans. Naturally, I thought of you and this house."

"Naturally. So, when is it? On Halloween?"

"Nope. Tuesday, the twenty-first. From 5 to 9 p.m. So, what do you say, Cleo? Can I count on you and Bertram?"

"Somebody else dropped out, didn't they?"

"You got me, Cleo. But your house is great. Come on, do it for the Historical Society. Pretty please?"

Oh, no. Not the begging. Not the puppy-dog eyes. Marty knew how to penetrate my defenses. It was the only thing of mine he could penetrate, bless his gay little heart.

"All right. We'll do it."

"Great! I knew I could count on you, Cleo." He unfolded the paper in his hand and passed it to me. "Fill out this bio and fax it to me by tomorrow. I need to upload it onto our website ASAP."

I sneaked a peek at the questionnaire.

Year built?

Who originally owned your home?

Are there any ghost stories associated with your house? Any special possessions significant to the house?

Marty was saying, "You can decorate for Halloween or not. Whatever you're comfortable doing. But, sugar, I recommend you ditch

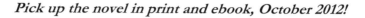

the Velvet Elvis. That's what I call truly scary."

Pick up the novel in print and ebook, October 2012!

Or find out more about Susan Abel Sullivan and
The Haunted Housewives of Allister, Alabama
at WorldWeaverPress.com.

ABOUT THE AUTHORS

Amanda C. Davis is a combustion engineer who loves baking, gardening, and low-budget horror films. Her short fiction has appeared in *Shock Totem, Orson Scott Card's InterGalactic Medicine Show*, and others. You can follow her on Twitter @davisac1 or read more of her work at www.amandacdavis.com.

A. E. Decker is a former ESL tutor, doll-maker, and historian determined to build a career as a full-time writer. She holds degrees in English and History and is a graduate of the Odyssey Writing Workshop. At present she is editing an anthology for the Bethlehem Writers' Group, writing the occasional short story, and working on a novel about a tomato-obsessed hit man of the supernatural.

Larry Hodges, of Germantown, MD, is an active member of SFWA with over 60 short story sales, over 40 since 2008. His story was the unanimous grand prize winner at the 2010 GSHW Story Competition. He's a 2006 Odyssey Writing Workshop graduate, a full-time writer with six books and over 1300 published articles in over 130 different publications, and a member of the USA Table Tennis Hall of Fame. Visit him at www.larryhodges.org.

British author, **Sue Houghton**, had her first short story published in 2001 and has since become a regular contributor to most of the women's magazines in the UK and around the world. She has written for ezines and given quotes for several publications on the art of creative writing. Her work has won competitions and her stories have appeared in seven anthologies. Sue's dream is to have her novel published. www.suehoughton.co.uk

Andrea Janes lives in Brooklyn, New York. From her front window she can see Upper New York Bay, a Victorian cemetery, and a high-voltage ConEd substation. She loves ghost stories, all things nautical, and tremendously big breakfasts. www.andreajanes.com

Terence Kuch is a consultant, novelist, and avid hiker. His writing has appeared in *Commonweal, Diagram, Dissent, New York magazine, North American Review, Slow Trains, Washington Post Book World, Washington Post Magazine*, etc., and has been anthologized by Random House and McGraw-Hill. A world traveler, his literary and speculative fiction has been published in the U.S., U.K., Canada, Australia, India, and Thailand. www.terencekuch.net

Robbie MacNiven is a small-time author and freelance journalist living in the Highlands of Scotland and currently enrolled as a full-time student at the University of Edinburgh, studying History and English Language. In between exams (only a passing discomfort) and writing Robbie follows politics, football, backstabs people on Team Fortress 2 and stalks small presses online to see if they have a "submit" button. He generally prefers cats to dogs, and is 20 years old.

Kou K. Nelson lives with her husband and dogs in the way East Bay of Northern California. She enhances her history degree by visiting cities that treasure their past, St. John's, Newfoundland, among them. She shared her love of history by teaching high school social studies for 15 years. She now owns her own dog training business, but continues to immerse herself in days of yore by attending period costume balls and various folk festivals. www.kouknelson.com

Jamie Rand is currently working toward his MFA at Virginia Tech. He has stories published in *Absinthe Revival, Blood Lotus, carte blanche*, and *Annalemma Magazine*. He also has a short story in the anthology *Best New Writing 2011*.

Shannon Robinson's work has appeared or is forthcoming in *Nimrod, Sycamore Review, Crab Creek Review, Sou'wester, New Ohio Review, Prick of the Spindle*, and *New Stories for the Midwest*. Recent honors include the

Katherine Anne Porter Prize, an Elizabeth George Foundation grant, and a Hedgebrook Fellowship. She holds an MFA from Washington University in St. Louis, and this past fall was the Writer-in-Residence at Interlochen Center for the Arts.

Calie Voorhis is a life-long fanatic of the fantastic, with stories in *Ray Gun Revival, Beyond Centauri, Fusion Fragment*, and *The Online Anathema Anthology*, and stories in the print anthologies *Dead Set: A Zombie Anthology, Space Sirens, Farspace 2, DOA - Tales of Extreme Terror, Andromeda Spaceways Inflight Magazine* - Issue 51, and *Anywhere but Earth*, among others. She holds a BS in Biology from UNC-Chapel Hill, an MFA in Writing Popular Fiction from Seton Hill University, and is an Odyssey Writing Workshop alumna.

Jay Wilburn is a public school teacher in beautiful Conway, South Carolina, where he lives with his wife and two sons. He has published many horror and speculative fiction stories. His first novel, *Loose Ends: A Zombie Novel*, is available now. He is a columnist for Dark Eclipse and for Perpetual Motion Machine Press. Follow his many dark thoughts at JayWilburn.com and @AmongTheZombies on Twitter.

Kristina Wojtaszek grew up as a woodland sprite and mermaid, playing around the shores of Lake Michigan. She earned a BA in Wildlife Management as an excuse to spend her days lost in the woods with a book in hand. She currently resides in the high desert country of Wyoming with her husband and two small children. She is fascinated by fairy tales and fantasy and her favorite haunts are libraries and cemeteries. Her novella *Opal* a unique twist on the tale of Snow White, comes out this November. authorkw.wordpress.com

About the Editor

Eileen Wiedbrauk, Editor-in-Chief of World Weaver Press, is an editor, writer, collegiate English instructor, blogger, coffee addict, cat herder, MFA graduate, fantasist-turned-fabalist-turned-urban-fantasy-junkie, Odyssey Writing Workshop alumna, photographer, designer, tech geek, entrepreneur, avid reader, and a somewhat decent cook. She wears many hats, as the saying goes. Which is an odd saying in this case, as she rarely looks good in hats. Her creative work has appeared in *North American Review, Swink, Enchanted Conversation*, and others. Her website, *Speak Coffee to Me*, can be found at eileenwiedbrauk.com.

Also Available from World Weaver Press

SHARDS OF HISTORY

Rebecca Roland

"Fast-paced, high-stakes drama in a fresh fantasy world. Rebecca Roland is a newcomer to watch!"
— James Maxey, author of *Greatshadow: The Dragon Apocalypse.*

Like all Taakwa, Malia fears the fierce winged creatures known as Jeguduns who live in the cliffs surrounding her valley. When the river dries up and Malia is forced to scavenge farther from the village than normal, she discovers a Jegudun, injured and in need of help.

Malia's existence—her status as clan mother in training, her marriage, her very life in the village—is threatened by her choice to befriend the Jegudun. But she's the only Taakwa who knows the truth: that the threat to her people is much bigger and much more malicious than the Jeguduns who've lived alongside them for decades. Lurking on the edge of the valley is an Outsider army seeking to plunder and destroy the Taakwa , and it's only a matter of time before the Outsiders find a way through the magic that protects the valley—a magic that can only be created by Taakwa and Jeguduns working together.

Now Malia is in a race against time. She must warn the Jeguduns that the Taakwa march against them and somehow convince the Taakwa that their real enemy isn't who they think it is before the Outsiders find a way into the valley and destroy everything she holds dear.

Available now!

CURSED: WICKEDLY FUN STORIES

Susan Abel Sullivan

"Quirky, clever, and just a little savage, *Cursed* is a delightful read!"
— Lane Robins, critically acclaimed author of *Maledicte* and *Kings and Assassins*

A young adult collection of four wickedly fun short stories featuring witches, werewolves, limericks that can change fate, and a sinister vine bent on murder and the destruction of Alabama! Inside quirky settings with creepy plots, characters discover new and unsettling powers as their worst fears manifest. You'll laugh, you'll shudder—you'll think twice about taking a deal from a bucktoothed woman.

Available now!

OPAL
a novella

Kristina Wojtaszek

From the novella: *These are but stories, stretched beyond death, like time itself, ever changing us, but themselves unchanged ...*

A gorgeous twisting of Snow White reminiscent of the lyrical tales of Patricia McKillip and Robin McKinney.

Coming November 2012.

☠

Made in the USA
San Bernardino, CA
09 November 2012